CLOSE ENCOUNTERS OF THE DEADLY KIND

Also by Joanne Pence

Ancient Secrets Series

ANCIENT ECHOES - ANCIENT SHADOWS

ANCIENT ILLUSIONS - ANCIENT DECEPTIONS

ANCIENT PASSAGES

The Donnelly Cabin Inn

IF I LOVED YOU - THIS CAN'T BE LOVE

SENTIMENTAL JOURNEY - A CERTAIN SMILE

TIME AFTER TIME

The Rebecca Mayfield Mysteries

ONE O'CLOCK HUSTLE - TWO O'CLOCK HEIST

THREE O'CLOCK SÉANCE - FOUR O'CLOCK SIZZLE

FIVE O'CLOCK TWIST - SIX O'CLOCK SILENCE

SEVEN O'CLOCK TARGET - EIGHT O'CLOCK SPLIT

NINE O'CLOCK RETREAT - THE 13th SANTA (Novella)

The Cook and Inspector Mysteries

DEATH ON A SILVER PLATTER - A QUICHE BEFORE DYING - THE MARINARA MURDERS -

CLOSE ENCOUNTERS OF THE DEADLY KIND

Others

SEEMS LIKE OLD TIMES - DANGEROUS JOURNEY

DANCE WITH A GUNFIGHTER - THE DRAGON'S LADY

THE GHOST OF SQUIRE HOUSE

CLOSE ENCOUNTERS OF THE DEADLY KIND

THE COOK AND INSPECTOR MYSTERIES

JOANNE PENCE

QUAIL HILL PUBLISHING

Copyright © 2024 by Joanne Pence

All rights reserved.

No part of this book may be reproduced in any form or by any electronic or mechanical means, including information storage and retrieval systems, without written permission from the author, except for the use of brief quotations in a book review.

This is a work of fiction. Names, characters, places, public or private institutions, corporations, towns, and incidents are the product of the author's imagination or are used fictitiously. Any resemblance to actual events, locales, or persons, living or dead, is coincidental.

Quail Hill Publishing

Eagle, ID 83616

Visit our website at www.quailhillpublishing.net

First Quail Hill Publishing E-book: July 2024

First Quail Hill Print Book: July 2024

CLOSE ENCOUNTERS OF THE DEADLY KIND

1

Patrol cars blocked the main entrance to Sigmund Stern Grove, their flashing red and blue lights blurred and garish in the early morning mist The rare June rainstorm that caused the residents of San Francisco to believe they'd been transported eight hundred miles north to Seattle had stopped for the moment.

Homicide Inspector Paavo Smith, tall and stern, in his midthirties with a lean, narrow-hipped build, followed a pathway through stands of eucalyptus and pine. His hair was dark brown, and his angular face was as unreadable as his icy blue eyes. Behind him and to his left was his partner, Homicide Inspector Toshiro Yoshiwara, called "Yosh," in his late thirties with short-cropped black hair, and a thick, muscular neck. Their oxfords sank deep into the drenched mud, creating suction they had to fight against, as if the earth itself wanted to hold them back. Neither spoke.

Under the broad umbrella-like expanse of a weeping willow hovered a small crowd of morning joggers and dogwalkers. Their expressions were hollow and fearful, different from the curious, excited looks usually worn by crime-scene witnesses. Just off the path, a police officer bent low over the bushes. One hand was jammed against a tree trunk, and a harsh gagging sound erupted from his throat.

A police sergeant nodded at the inspectors and lifted the crime scene tape that stretched from tree to tree. He looked shaken, not like a police veteran who had seen a multitude of horrors. "The medical examiner hasn't arrived yet," he said, breathing deeply. "Neither has the CSU."

A patrolman stood guard over the body covered by a thin plastic tarp. The wet ground around the body was a mire of running shoe patterns and dog footprints. There was no blood, no flattened or torn grass or bushes, no sign that a death struggle had taken place here.

At the sergeant's nod, the patrolman reached down, gripped the edges of the tarp and drew away the covering. The two detectives stared down at the corpse.

"Good Christ." Yosh whispered under his breath. He turned his head.

Paavo remained impassive as he pulled a pair of latex gloves from his pocket and slipped them on, then stepped closer to study the victim.

The nude body was that of a male Caucasian, early forties or so, about five-foot-ten and thin. The skin was an opaque white. The man's hair was neatly razor cut; his hands free of calluses or stains, the skin soft, the nails manicured; toenails short, square-cut, no bunions or other effects of ill-fitting shoes. In short, all signs of a comfortable life. Until now.

A wide band of skin in the shape of the number seven had been removed from a pasty chest. Around the neck was a long, black nylon strap attached to a bulky black metal device that appeared to be a weird combination of binoculars and goggles.

But the main thing, the thing that had both hardened inspectors staring with a mixture of fascination and horror, was that the entire area from the pubis to the sigmoid colon had been cored out, leaving his pelvis a clean, bloodless cavity. No post-mortem lividity appeared on the part of the body pressed against the ground. The whole thing had a tidy, almost surreal appearance. Not only did no blood spatter the area, no blood was anywhere; apparently, not even in the victim. A gutted, empty shell.

Paavo glanced over at Yoshiwara, whose eyes betrayed no emotion. "Have you ever seen goggles like those?"

Yoshiwara studied them a moment before answering. "Never. The metal looks tarnished and old—like something out of World War Two, maybe."

"We'll run tests and send out inquiries, see if anyone knows what that thing is," Paavo said. "The one thing we do know, someone left it as a message."

Yoshiwara's gaze traveled over the mutilated corpse. "A message from a madman."

On a cliff facing the Pacific Ocean, nestled between the Presidio to the east and Lincoln Park on the west, lay one of San Francisco's most exclusive enclaves. Angelina Amalfi parked her white Ferrari Portofino in front of a stately gray mansion on Sea Cliff Avenue, on the ocean front side of the street. She was a young woman, age twenty-eight, with short, wavy dark brown hair that sported blond highlights.

At the white double entry doors, she rang the bell. After waiting, checking her French manicure, smoothing her businesslike gray and raspberry Ann Taylor suit, she rang again.

Finally, a middle-aged woman with perfectly coifed dyed blond hair opened the door. She was short and plump, and wore billowing slacks of blue silk, a matching over-blouse, and several rows of gold chains in a variety of weaves and sizes.

Heavy gold rings with diamonds and pearls graced nearly every finger.

With one such bejeweled finger, she fluffed her bangs as her mascara-ringed eyes surveyed Angie from head to toe. "Yeah?"

"Hello," Angie said cheerfully, holding out her hand. "I'm Angelina Amalfi. Fantasy Dinners. So happy to meet you." At the confused expression on the woman's face, Angie pulled back the hand she'd offered. "We have an appointment. That is, if you're Triana Crisswell?"

Angie had been running an ad in the *San Francisco Chronicle* for a week to promote her brand-new business. But so far, this was the only legitimate inquiry for a "fantasy dinner" that she'd received—as long as it wasn't a hoax.

"Hey, you're right, sweetie," Triana Crisswell said after a while. "God, am I forgetful or what? Don't just stand there, come on in." She pulled the door open wide and waited for Angie to enter. "So you're the gal with the cute little dinner business." She guided Angie across the entry hall to the living room. "When I saw your ad, it sounded like such fun. I'm so glad you had the time to see me. I know you've got to be real busy, what with running a business like that and all."

"I certainly am busy," Angie said. Maybe not with her new business, exactly, but in general, she was a busy person. Sort of. "But simply talking to you on the phone told me that you were a person I would like to do business with. I made it a point to find room in my schedule to see you." Especially since the schedule was empty.

"I appreciate it, sweetie," Triana said. "So, come on, sit down. I'll get us some coffee. You like coffee? I could make tea if you don't. Or maybe white wine?"

"Coffee would be fine," Angie replied.

"Just give me a minute," Triana Crisswell called as she disappeared down the hallway.

Angie settled back into a silk-upholstered chair. Although the front of the house, facing the street, had a traditional San Francisco style, the back wall of the living room had large windows overlooking the Pacific. Angie could barely make out the Farallon Islands in the distance. And beyond the islands, dark storm clouds loomed.

Just like in this business venture, Angie mused, as a bad feeling about being here suddenly struck for no apparent reason. Judging from the house, which included the lavish furniture and art work, if she was commissioned to put on a fantasy dinner party here, she shouldn't be stiffed for her fee. She tried her best to calm her new-business-owner-trying-to-make-a-good-impression nerves.

Triana Crisswell came back into the living room carrying a tray with two coffees, a creamer and sugar bowl. She put them on the table, handed Angie a cup and saucer, then sat back with her own and loudly slurped the brew. "Oh, my! Be careful. It's so hot I burned my tongue." She put down the cup and waved her hand as if to fan herself. "You're probably wondering what I'm doing in this big house without a servant. Oh, and you can call me Triana. What did you say your name was? I'm so forgetful sometimes!" Triana giggled, then continued, "But back to what I was saying, what would I do here all day with a servant? Of course, I have someone come in to clean, someone else to cook dinners—my husband is such a fuss-budget about his food—but other than that, I hate having some stranger underfoot all day, telling my husband what I do, who my friends are. You know what I mean?"

Angie's head swirled, trying to follow the conversation, then gave up. "You can call me Angie," she murmured once Triana stopped talking.

"Oh? Oh, right," Triana said. "So, Angie, tell me about your dinners."

Angie poured some cream into her coffee, then sat up

primly, her hands neatly folded in her lap, legs crossed at the ankles. "Well, as I mentioned on the phone, the idea behind Fantasy Dinners is to create a dinner party around a theme, whatever theme you would like. My staff and I take care of all the details, including hiring caterers to prepare the meal and serve it, helping guests with costumes if your party requires them, and generally creating the perfect setting for you. You tell me what your theme is, and your budget, and we'll build a fantasy to fulfill it."

Mrs. Crisswell giggled. "Build me a fantasy—my, my, doesn't that sound great! I tell you, my fantasies were hot and heavy when I was young, sweetie."

Hmm. Angie decided she needed to come up with a slightly different way to describe her business. Ignoring the suggestive remark, she placed her hand on the leather binder at her side. "In here are many ideas for dinners. For example, if you're interested in using ancient Rome as your theme, I can put on a dinner featuring food for the gods—nectar and ambrosia, as well as some modern Roman dishes such as *manicotti* or something fancier, like medallions of veal stuffed with crab meat, fontina and asparagus. Or whatever you'd like me to serve. We could drape fabric on the walls and ask your guests to wear togas. Plus, as a special feature, if you wish, I have a number of mystery plays that the guests could participate in. They are all variations on some basic mysteries. The Roman one, for example, is called 'Who Killed Nero?'"

"I don't know about all that." Triana scrunched her mouth. "People at my party might not care about who killed anybody."

Angie's spirits were rapidly sinking. Triana was strange, and this wasn't going well. "You don't need to request a mystery play at all. The fantasy dinner, alone, will be a wonderful event for your guests. Do you have a theme in mind?"

"Yes." Triana's eyes gazed upward. "We look to the future. After all, most of us have to live in the future."

"The future?" Angie, even more confused, glanced at the ceiling, where Triana still stared. "Ah, yes, the future!" she gushed, remembering the adage that 'the customer is always right.' "Of course. I love dinners that have to do with the future. They're my favorite fantasies!" Whatever they are.

Triana's eyes widened. "Really? You've done them before?"

"I've cooked lots of dinners. Past, future, present—you name it," Angie said. She wasn't lying either. She had cooked many dinners. Not a single Fantasy Dinner yet, but she was careful not to say she had. Anyway, she had to start somewhere.

"Well, that sounds perfect, sweetie."

"I'm glad to hear that." Angie breathed a little easier. "Now, why don't you tell me what our futuristic dinner is all about so I can begin planning a fabulous event?"

"It's for a group I belong to. The Prometheus Group. Prometheus was the fire and liver guy. Greek mythology, you know. Which might not sound futuristic, but it is. Anyway, these people are so smart, I can't tell you! I admire them so much." Triana stopped speaking and a dreamy look came over her. "The leader of the group is called Algernon. That's it, just one name. Anyway, he's written a book. So I want to have a party and invite important people from the media and bookstore owners and people who will buy the book from him. We'll feed them something so delicious they'll write good reviews, right? Don't you think that'll be a good thing?"

"I think that'll be a very good thing." Angie's head filled with the idea of serving an elegant meal to the *literati* of the Bay Area. This was the kind of interesting party she'd dreamed of when she came up with the idea for her Fantasy Dinners business.

Triana's expression turned all but lovestruck. "And our leader, Algernon, is so handsome! Like to die. Wait until you meet him! You'll want to pinch yourself to be sure you're awake.

Anyway, his book is coming out next month. Is that enough time to set up a launch party and book signing?"

"Absolutely!" Angie was thrilled. Along with Algernon's book, this could be exactly the sort of party that could launch her career as well. "When Fantasy Dinners takes charge, we handle everything on time, every time. Remember: 'Our business is your fantasy, not your nightmare.'" She'd come up with that motto, but it didn't have quite the right ring to it yet.

"The dinner will be held here at my home," Triana said. "I'll invite around fifty people. This house is large enough to accommodate them. I'll give you more details as we go along."

Fifty people? That was a bit more than she was expecting for her first Fantasy Dinner. But "never say never." That could be another motto she'd use for her business. "That will be fine," Angie said, working to keep any hesitancy out of her voice. "So, a fantasy about the future? Do you have a particular theme in mind, or should I develop one?"

"I want the dinner to bring Algernon's book to life. I want us to live what he's writing about."

"Oh, how interesting. What is his book?"

"It's called: *Life Beyond Mars—The Search for Extraterrestrial Life In Our Galaxy.* And you know what?"

Extraterrestrials? Angie's heart sank. How was she supposed to create a fantasy dinner about space aliens? To begin with, who knew what they ate? She glanced at Triana and realized the woman was waiting for her to respond.

"No, what?" she murmured.

"Algernon has proved it. He's proved that not only is there extraterrestrial life, but ... *they're here.*"

2

The Sigmund Stern Grove victim had no fingerprints on file, but running facial recognition against DMV records had come up with the match—Bertram Lambert, thirty-nine years old, five-foot-nine, one hundred sixty pounds, brown hair, hazel eyes. Address, 1551 O'Farrell Street, apartment 8.

When Paavo and Yosh went to the address, it proved to be an old one. Lambert's former landlady knew nothing about him except that he worked in the Bank of America's financial processing center.

The detectives contacted the bank. Lambert's supervisor, Henry Fisher, knew of no close friends or relatives nearby. On his employment forms, Lambert's address was still shown as the incorrect earlier one, and the only next of kin was a sister who lived in Iowa.

Paavo tried several times to reach her, but no one answered his call.

Finally, Fisher agreed to identify the body, and confirmed the dead man was Bertram Lambert.

After leaving the morgue, Paavo walked out to the parking lot with Fisher. In his experience, people who weren't close friends or relatives of the deceased often wanted to talk a bit after the emotional roller coaster of identifying a dead body.

Fisher, he quickly learned, fell into that camp.

Fisher put a cigarette in his mouth, then had trouble lighting it because of the way his hand was shaking. Finally, he drew in several deep puffs as if to rid his nose and lungs of the thick, stagnant air he'd been breathing. "I can't believe he's dead," Fisher murmured. "He was so quiet. No one could possibly want to hurt him."

Paavo nodded, and after a pause, gently asked, "Do you know anything about his personal life? Who his friends were? If he had any friends at work?"

Fisher shook his head. "I don't think he kept friends. He was, I don't know, too clingy. At work, he came on too strong, overwhelming people with questions about their private lives until they felt smothered and backed off. It seemed he was always looking for friends, but I don't know if he ever found any."

"Why not?"

Fisher shrugged. "He never said, and I never asked." He sighed. "I always saw Bert as a prime candidate for some wacko cult. You know, like that old Heaven's Gate group where they all killed themselves to fly up to some comet."

"Do you know if he found any groups or clubs to join?"

"Not that I heard. I'll ask around at work, but the guy was—hell, I suppose I shouldn't say now that he's gone—but the guy was boring. He led a dull life and told people all about it until they just stopped listening. At least, I stopped."

"I'd appreciate whatever you could find out," Paavo said.

"Sure. It's funny, though, after trying so hard..."

"Funny?" Paavo prodded.

Fisher's gaze was dull. "Considering the way he died, I guess he finally found somebody who took an interest in him."

Back at his desk in Homicide, Paavo found a message saying

the autopsy wouldn't be performed until the next day at one o'clock. Without either relatives or the press clamoring for results, the autopsy had to wait its turn. A determination as to the cause of death, at least, would help give some idea of the type of killer they were dealing with.

No defensive wounds had been observed on the body. The victim had to have been subdued, maybe dead, before the mutilations began. The questions, therefore, remained: how was he killed? And why?

There had to be a reason he'd been murdered and carved like a Thanksgiving turkey ready for stuffing, and someone had to know what it was.

Paavo reread the crime scene unit's report. Not only had the body been drained of blood, but it had been washed clean. Dried soap residue had been found on the hair and in the ear canals. The assumption was that the victim had been bathed, then wrapped in plastic sheeting of some kind and transported to the park. Not a single stray fiber or hair had been found.

Paavo shook his head at the weirdness of the report. He'd never dealt with a Mr. Clean or Molly Maid killer before.

"No. Never. No way. Forget it. Is that clear enough?" Connie Rogers jabbed her spoon into her tiramisu, scooped up some of the layered mascarpone cream, chocolate, and espresso-soaked ladyfingers, and ate it.

Angie knew better than to respond immediately. She hadn't shown up at Connie's gift shop, Everyone's Fancy, bearing tiramisu, eclairs, a raspberry mousse, and non-fat lattes, to argue, but to cajole Connie into helping her set up a space-alien Fantasy Dinner.

Connie wasn't pleased with the idea. Without comment,

Angie took a bite of an éclair and waited for Connie's inevitable guilt to begin.

The two had met in the course of the investigation of the murder of Connie's younger sister and, although opposite in almost every way, quickly grew close. Where Angie, age twenty-eight, was slim, brunette and single, Connie, age thirty-two, was a little overweight, blonde and divorced. Angie had a college degree, traveled widely, and was well versed in art and literature. Connie graduated from high school, had never left the U.S., and picked up whatever knowledge of art and literature she had from romantic movies on TV. On the other hand, Connie was a savvy businesswoman and owned a small, successful gift shop called Everyone's Fancy, while Angie struggled to find, and keep, a job in the culinary field she loved.

"It could really be a lot of fun," Angie said with softly voiced encouragement.

Angie had arrived at the gift shop at two in the afternoon, the time Connie referred to as the shop's mid-afternoon doldrums—the hours between the lunchtime window shoppers and the after-work rush. She and Connie sat at a small table in the shop's back office. The door was left open so they could see and hear if anyone entered the store. No one did, which gave Angie the opportunity to explain her new business to Connie, and to ask for help, which she promptly did.

As Connie sipped the Starbucks non-fat latte Angie had brought her and then took another bite of tiramisu, she gave Angie glances that said she knew exactly what Angie was up to. Without a word, Angie spooned the mousse into two paper cups and gave one to Connie.

"You know," Angie added, "this UFO stuff is all the rage now. Not only have I fallen into something new and exciting, but I'm willing to share it with you."

"You've fallen, all right. Head first. It's insane."

"It's a job," Angie stated, her tone strident. But then she sat back, realizing she sounded desperate. Although, why shouldn't she be? She needed success at something in her life.

After Connie finished her tiramisu, she said, "If you want my advice, you'll start your business with something you understand. What do you know about extra-terrestrials or this Prometheus Group? They're probably a bunch of crackpots." She pushed the cup of mousse back toward Angie's napkin, as if to show she wasn't one to be bought by sweets. She then peered out the door to see if any customers had managed to sneak in without causing the entry bell to bong. The store remained empty.

"It's precisely because I don't know that much about them, or their beliefs," Angie reasoned, "that I need your help. All I have to do is to create a dinner party for them, not join them. I want it to be a very special dinner. After all, I didn't name my new business Fantasy Dinners for nothing."

Connie fiddled with some envelopes on the table. They looked like bills. "What did you say your motto was? 'Your fantasy is my nightmare.' Was that it?"

"Ha, ha." Angie frowned. "I have no idea why you're taking this attitude." She tasted the mousse. It might have been made from hair gel for all the enjoyment it gave her. She shoved it aside.

"And who's this Algernon guy?" Connie reached for the cup of mousse Angie had spooned out for her. "What kind of name is that? It might not be so bad if it was his last name. Maybe not if it was his first name. But his *only* name? He's not exactly famous."

"It's stylistic license. He's supposed to be *very* good looking."

"Anyone pretentious enough to use just one name had better be." As Connie tasted the mousse, her eyes rolled blissfully.

Time to try again, Angie thought. "Seriously, Connie, I wish you'd help me. Now that I've accepted the job, I've got to make something of it. I need to find out about aliens or extraterrestrials or ETs or whatever they're called. Have you ever heard what they supposedly eat?"

Connie did a double take. "No."

"Me neither." Angie thought a moment. "Step one has to be to find out what the lore is about aliens—what people who believe in them say they eat so I can serve it—or some edible version of it. Whatever it is. I think that would make a fun Fantasy Dinner, don't you?"

"That depends on what food you come up with," Connie said, polishing off the mousse. "If it's bugs, even more I'll have nothing to do with this."

Angie sighed wearily, worrying that Connie might be right. "All I've ever heard about space and food is that the moon's made out of green cheese."

"Green cheese?" Connie sneered, reaching for an eclair. "And here I'd always thought moon pies were the real thing."

Angie suddenly brightened. "You may be on to something. For instance, there are Rocket Popsicles, Mars candy bars and Milky Ways. For those who can't eat chocolate, there are always Starbursts. I could have a bunch of that sort of stuff spread around for the guests to munch on."

Connie rolled her eyes. "Yeah right, and while you're at it, you can play 'Fly Me to the Moon' as your music selection."

"Oh, no! I haven't even thought about music! But there's also 'Moon River' and 'Blue Moon.'"

"I was joking!" Connie said. "Although the more I hear about this, 'Bad Moon Rising' sounds more appropriate. What does Paavo say about it?"

Angie's smile suddenly vanished. She had to swallow a few times before she found her voice. "I don't know. I haven't told him about it."

Connie stared at her. "Do you mean to tell me you and he

still aren't seeing each other? What's going on, Angie? This is crazy."

Angie's jaw quivered slightly. "He's been busy, and now I am as well."

"I know you don't mean that," Connie said softly. "Call him. Talk this through. You're crazy about him!"

"I can't do that. I know when a guy's no longer interested," Angie said, her chin high as she stood. "A customer just came into the store. Time for me to leave anyway. Please think about helping me with my Fantasy Dinner. I have the feeling I'm going to need all the help I can get."

That evening, a short, chubby booth attendant stood at a table filled with brochures about UFOs. He waved his arms and loudly called out to the crowd milling about in front of the Moscone Center, where a big science fiction and fantasy convention was being held. "My friends! Come and learn about our movement to find safety in a new world. Discover all that the government isn't telling you. Beware! The end of mankind is fast approaching!"

A man, unwashed and dressed in several layers of clothes so soiled they practically stood up on their own, walked up to the table. He pointed to the cardboard sign in front of the attendant.

New members! Free drawings!
$100 to the lucky winner! Join today!

"What do I have to do to be in the drawing?" he asked.

The attendant frowned at the man's appearance. "It's usually five bucks, which is deducted from the price of your ticket."

"I got no money for a ticket," the fellow said.

The attendant handed him a cheap BIC. "Okay. Just fill out a card."

With painstaking slowness, the man filled out the card, then handed it back. The attendant glanced at the address: a Salvation Army kitchen. Homeless. It figured. Then at the name: Felix Rolfe.

He stared. It was familiar... Felix Rolfe.

Finally, the attendant smiled. "Good luck."

3

The next morning, Angie was no closer to an idea for an out-of-this-world dinner party than she had been the night before. But she had three and a half weeks before the event, so she wasn't too worried. Yet.

She sat on the sofa in her living room, her coffee on an end table, reading the morning *Chronicle* on her computer tablet. From her apartment high atop Russian Hill, she could see the northern part of the city and the bay beyond. Rain was falling, casting a gray gloom over the view.

She wished Paavo was with her. She had never before felt about anyone the way she did him. She'd thought she'd been "in love" several times in her life, but it was always a fun, easy, kind of love—loving dates, parties, good times. And when she grew bored or met someone else who seemed to be more fun, off she'd go with her newest "love." So, yes, when she was young and foolish, she'd acted young and foolish.

With Paavo, that had changed. She had changed. There was nothing "easy" about loving him. And instead of running from him when life became difficult, those times only served to help her learn more about the full measure of the man, and caused her feelings to deepen.

Unfortunately, he didn't feel the same way. Two months earlier, a frightening, horrible killer—the man who had murdered Connie's sister—had gone after Angie, captured her, and tried to kill her. The experience had terrified her, leaving her afraid to be alone. Paavo had opened his home and his heart to her. She'd stayed with him for nearly three weeks, in his home and in his bed, until she had gathered the strength to go back to her own apartment.

If he'd asked her to move in with him, she probably would have, even though they hadn't known each other for especially long as far as months went, but their time together had been intense. There was a saying that "there are days when weeks happen." That was how life had been with Paavo.

But then he changed.

After she returned to her own apartment, he continued to see her at first. But as time went on, their dates became less and less frequent. Now, he no longer called or visited.

When she phoned him, he was always too busy to see her. He used to find time in the past, but now, no more. And, and she had no idea why. She wracked her brain for what she had done that was so wrong, but couldn't come up with anything.

She could only guess he had decided she wasn't the right woman for him. He had never actually said that he loved her. She was well aware of that, and so held back from telling him how she felt since she had always heard such declarations could scare a man off. Was it true? She had no idea. At times, she was tempted to call him and tell him she loved him, but everything she knew about him told her that was not the way to bring him back to her.

She decided to simply act as if they were friends. Nothing more. If that was all he wanted to be, could she accept it? Perhaps being his friend was better than not seeing him at all.

So many times, back when she had believed they were "a couple," just hearing his deep voice had set her mind somewhat at ease. After all, he was a cop, a crazy dangerous job. As a detective, he wore street clothes, but she'd learned, firsthand, that didn't matter when danger came to call. She had watched him get shot; she had watched him shoot a man. Fear for his safety, she had come to realize, would always be with her.

For that reason, as a friend, she should continue to call him now and then. "No hard feelings," that would be her personal motto.

Finally, she turned back to her Fantasy Dinner and forced herself to concentrate on it.

What kind of designs should she use? Astrology? No, these people, she was sure, considered themselves scientific and would look down on astrology. Theirs might be pseudo-science to some, but she guessed many were serious students of technology, not dilettantes of the paranormal.

She stood, folding her arms within the long kimono sleeves of her pink silk robe, and began to pace. She needed a theme that was both exceptional and unique. Something that perhaps the general public didn't know about.

So, who did?

A shave-and-a-haircut knock sounded at her door. She knew that knock and knew it was not bringing the answer to her question.

Angie opened the door to greet her across-the-hall neighbor, Stanfield Bonnette, a tall, blond, youthful-looking fellow. He should be at work, not standing here casually dressed in off-white linen slacks and a loose-fitting forest green shirt. As much as he thought of himself as an up-and-coming bank executive, from what Angie saw of his work ethic, down-and-going was a more apt description.

"I didn't know this was a bank holiday," she said, stepping back so he could enter.

"I had a migraine this morning." He did his best to feign suffering. "It's gone now. I was wondering if you wanted to go to a movie. The Castro's showing a rerun of the old classic, *Plan 9 From Outer Space*. It's a hoot. I've watched it a few times on TV, and seeing it on a big screen could be fun."

"I don't have time, I'm afraid," she said.

He walked into the kitchen. "I haven't heard you mention your cop friend for a while, so if he's chasing dead bodies instead of yours—I mean, instead of taking you out—why not come? It won't take that much time."

"I'm trying to start up a new business and it's time-consuming." She followed him. "*Outer Space*, you said? Actually, for my Fantasy Dinner business, I need to learn something about extraterrestrials, and maybe even UFOs."

"UFOs? What are you planning on cooking? Space cookies?"

He went over to her espresso machine. "Ah! It's still on."

"Have a cup. Actually, I'll need to learn more about twenty-first century high-tech, not twentieth century B-movies using pie-pans for flying saucers. I need help sorting through all the UFO and alien stuff that's out there."

"I guess I'm just an old-fashioned kind of guy," he said, opening her cookie jar. "Oh, looky there! Chocolate-covered macaroons. My favorite. Home-made?"

"Yes. Help yourself."

He was already reaching into the jar. "What does your hot-shot cop friend think about this business of yours?" He bit into the cookie. "Mmm. Fabulous."

"I haven't had a chance to tell him."

Stan actually stopped eating to look at her with one eyebrow lifted as if to say he knew there was more to the story. "Well, given all your acquaintances, I should think at least one would know about UFOs and such. They're so in." He then took another bite of the macaroon.

She pondered that a moment. "You may be ri ... yes! You *are* right!" She smacked the heel of her hand to her forehead. "How could I have forgotten?"

She dashed to the den. Stan grabbed another cookie and followed, watching as she picked up her cellphone from her desk. "What are you doing?" he asked.

"I just remembered an old boyfriend, an astrophysicist. He can tell me about UFOs."

"An astrophysicist?" He gawked at the number of contacts in her phone as she scrolled through them. "Are all those old boyfriends?"

"Of course not! Not even half are. Ah, here he is—Derrick Holton."

She sat down on the white iron daybed across from her desk and stared at the name on her phone. Memories of how thrilled she had been to have attracted the attention of such a handsome astrophysicist came back to her. Derrick had been a rising star who had worked at NASA, no less, and last she heard, was teaching at UC Berkeley. Her parents had been ecstatic that she was seeing him. She and Derrick had dated for four months, but the relationship was far more serious on his part than hers.

Stan sat on the daybed beside her. "Well, if he's an astrophysicist, I can see why you dumped him. He was probably old, stodgy and boring."

"Actually, he was young and good-looking. But he wanted to get married. It was a few years back. I was only twenty-three or so, and much more interested in living in Paris for a while. Which I did. He took the hint, and that was that."

Stan's eyebrows lifted. "He wanted to marry you? You were that close to him?"

"We were close, yes." Instead of hitting the call button, she put her phone down.

Stan stared at the phone a moment too long. "I think you

did the right thing," he said firmly. "You wouldn't have been happy with a guy like that. Serious, possessive, head in the clouds. You need someone down to earth and fun."

"Like Paavo," she murmured, more to herself than Stan.

"Oh, now there's a barrel of laughs!" Stan tightened his lips into a pout. "Someday, Angie, you'll open your eyes and discover the jewel right under your very nose."

"Forget it, Stan." She headed back to the living room taking her phone with her. Stan followed like a puppy.

"You're breaking my heart," he said.

"Have another macaroon." She flicked her thumb toward the kitchen.

"I will. Anyway, I don't think it's a good idea to call an old boyfriend. He might get the wrong impression. It could be awkward for you both."

"I'll have to make my purpose clear." She dropped onto the sofa.

Stan called out from the kitchen over the rattle of the cookie jar's lid. "Still, to call a NASA scientist and ask him about UFOs could be taken as an insult."

"Derrick's not that way. And if he doesn't know about them, I'm sure he'd point me in the right direction."

"Well, I think you're just asking for trouble." Balancing a stack of four oversized cookies in the palm of one hand, Stan opened the front door to leave. He glanced back at Angie. "If you won't listen to me about this, talk to the cop."

She couldn't imagine any reason to tell Paavo about Derrick. In fact, that was the last thing she wanted to do. Of course, if he was the jealous type... But he wasn't, which was a good thing. Usually. "I can handle this on my own, Stan. Paavo's much too busy to deal with UFOs."

4

So far, the only clues Paavo had to work with to solve Bertram Lambert's murder were the bizarre style of the mutilation, the number seven on the man's chest, and the mysterious goggles. He'd been looking online at military gear catalogues and manuals to try to find a similar type of goggle, but so far, no luck.

But then he got a call from Ray Falco, a criminologist in CSI. He had been working on the goggles and found a partial fingerprint on the inside of the metal casing, as if someone had taken the casing off at some point to clean or repair the interior. "We found a match to the print," he said. "Myron Ramsbottom."

Ramsbottom? "Is that a CSI joke?" Paavo asked.

"Nope. It's a legit family name. But the guy dropped off our radar some twenty years ago. He must've changed his name."

"Or killed himself," Yosh muttered.

They took the information and pulled up a photo of a young, good-looking fellow with black hair and brown eyes. They would work on finding out who and where he was now, but they had to recognize the possibility that the fingerprint was, itself, decades old.

Paavo once again tried to reach Lambert's sister in Iowa, and this time she answered the call.

"My brother never married," Janice Hazan said with a slight sniffle shortly after Paavo broke the news of her brother's murder. "He spent most of his first thirty-five years here in Ottumwa. He traveled a little, but kept coming back home." She sniffled again. "But then, two years ago, he moved to San Francisco. It was the happiest thing he ever did, or so he said. Every day since, I knew he would end up this way. I felt it in my bones. I warned him, over and over, to come back home. Would he listen to me? Not one bit! But that was Bertram for you."

"Where else did he live?" Paavo asked.

"Oh, he tried Phoenix, Albuquerque, even Las Vegas and some small towns in Nevada. He liked the southwest, but it didn't like him."

"Do you know why he moved to San Francisco?" Paavo asked.

"I never understood it. My brother used his inheritance to buy himself a little house," Hazan said. "Paid way too much for it, if you ask me. He lived alone. Just a sec—it's on my phone. Okay, the address is 91 Seventh Avenue. I understand it was a nice enough place. Not that he ever invited me. Oh, well, too late for regrets now, isn't it?"

"I'm sorry, Mrs. Hazan, to have to ask you these questions at a time like this," Paavo said, although the woman hardly sounded broken up. "As next of kin, if we could have your permission to enter the home—"

"Of course," she said brusquely. "I know you'll get in there one way or the other so why not speed things up? Just don't mess it up too much, that's all I ask. I guess I'll have to come see it, since it'll be mine, now."

"I'm sure that's up to you. No one here seems to know of any friends or close acquaintances of your brother's. Do you know of any?"

"Bertram wasn't the sort to make friends. That was why he kept coming back to Ottumwa. He said he went to San Francisco to join the city's swinging single scene, but I knew it wouldn't work for him. He wasn't the easiest man to like. A bit on the dull side. For him, winning a pittance in a lottery was exciting. Poor guy. Oh, well. What can I say?"

"We couldn't find a car registered to him. Do you know if he had one?"

"I think he sold it a year or two ago. Said there was nowhere to park in the city so he was better off without it. He used a bicycle to get around. Or the bus."

Paavo nodded. He had to fight the urge to hurry through routine questions about friends, men or women, clubs, interests, threats, changes in attitude or worries. She had no information about any of that.

"I see." This line of questioning was getting nowhere. "Your brother was found with goggles that we suspect are old and of military origin. Do you know about them or anything like them?"

"No."

"Was your brother ever in the military, or have interest in military kinds of things?"

"Not hardly. He despised everything that had to do with the military or killing. He was kind of a wimp, to tell the truth."

"Thank you, Mrs. Hazan. I'll call you as soon as we learn anything." Paavo was glad to hang up. So much for the woman's brotherly love.

He checked the time and hurried down to the medical examiner's laboratory.

There, Paavo put on a paper gown, mask, and booties for the autopsy. Despite the industrial strength disinfectant, the stench from the body permeated the room.

"I see some of my work's already been done for me," Ramirez said as she studied the body. "The first bit of information you need to know is the man had been dead two days before his body was discovered. And since he was found on a fairly popular part of the Grove, we can assume he was left there shortly before the discovery."

The ME then needed to make an incision. Normally, Ramirez didn't hesitate before making the first slightly rounded incision from shoulder to shoulder, and the next straight down to the groin. Except this time, there was no groin.

Ramirez drew in her breath and ran the scalpel across the shoulders and then from the breastbone downward until she ran out of flesh. She removed the rib cage to reveal the liver, heart, lungs, and other organs of a non-smoker in good health. No ruptures or puncture marks. Not until she cut around the back of Lambert's head and peeled the skin away did she find cracks in the skull, and after the cranium was removed, a broken brain stem. The trauma and shatter pattern on the skull indicated that a powerful blow to the head was the likely cause of death.

The results of tests on what body fluids the ME could find would come later, along with Ramirez's conclusions as to the type of blade used to make the precise cuts on the body. The wounds, she noted, had been cauterized, which made no sense. Paavo had left the autopsy with more questions than he'd had when he'd entered it.

Back at his desk, he listened to a voice mail from Angie. She said she realized they hadn't talked in a while and wondered how he was doing. She mentioned that she was working on developing a new business for herself and it was taking up all her time. She ended with, "Stay safe out there."

He'd spent so many years with scarcely anyone concerned about where he was or what he was doing, it was still hard for him to realize that Angie not only cared, but worried about him. The novelty of that, of knowing her and loving her, had been a good feeling. Too good.

He stared at the phone a while, wanting to call her back, but finally deciding not to.

Two months ago, one of his cases nearly got her killed. It had been all his fault. As time passed and he had gotten over the initial shock, the more he thought about it, the more he realized he had to end it with her. He made her life too dangerous.

Even his case before that had put her in danger since she became curious about something in it and had jumped in with both feet, naïve, and not wary or cautious enough.

As much as he loved being with her, he couldn't live with himself if she were hurt or, God forbid, killed because of him. That was reality and he couldn't change it.

He should have just quit her cold turkey—cut her out of his life all at once. But he knew that would hurt her, and he would hate himself even more than he already did. So he cut back on calls, visits, and dates, until, now, it had been a full week since they'd spoken.

And he'd hated every minute of it. He played her message again, just to hear her voice. She sounded upbeat. Maybe she'd gotten over him already. His plan was working. He should feel great about it.

Instead, he felt miserable.

But at the moment he needed to get his head back into this case. He put his phone aside and rubbed his temples.

The callousness of Bertram Lambert's murder preyed upon him. The murder had an almost ritualistic tinge to it. And rituals had a way of repeating themselves, over and over.

"Hello."

The warm timbre of Derrick Holton's voice over the telephone line was exactly as Angie remembered it, and it hurled her back to the time when they'd first met. He had possessed a ready smile and used to act on her every whim, remember her every word, and dote on her like a man possessed. He had always been there when she needed him, not off somewhere dealing with dead bodies and murderers.

Why hadn't she appreciated him more? At the time they dated, she had obviously enjoyed the adventures around her more than she'd enjoyed Derrick. But he really was a pretty special guy.

"Hi, Derrick. This is Angie Amalfi."

Silence. Had he forgot her that quickly? Her hand tightened on her cellphone and she sat down on the yellow Hepplewhite chair in her living room. "Remember me?" she asked.

"Of... of course! Angelina, is it really you? I'm breathless."

I'm breathless. That was a very Derrick-like elegant turn of phrase. The sort of phrase Paavo wouldn't have used if a gun were put to his head. "It's really me," she said, trying to put a cheerful, friendly lilt to her voice. "I'm sorry to bother you after all this time, but I was hoping you might spare a few minutes to help me with a project. I just have a few questions."

"Of course I can! Are you back in San Francisco?"

She noticed he was as quick to want to help her as ever, which caused her to feel both good but also worried about what that might mean. "Yes, I'm here. And I don't need much of your time, if it wouldn't be a problem for you, that is."

"A problem? No ... no, not at all. As a matter of fact, if you're free tomorrow evening, why don't we meet for an early dinner? I have to go to a lecture at eight-thirty in the south of Market area. Before that I'd love to meet and talk with you."

"Dinner?" She wasn't sure about that. There were certain implications about having dinner with an old boyfriend, such as, it smacked of a date. "I only need to ask you a few questions.

Nothing more. And I'm sure it won't take long. Coffee somewhere would be fine. I don't want to waste your time."

There was a lengthy pause. "It's no waste of time." His voice was low, and for the first time, sounded truly sincere, sounded like the Derrick she'd once known, and had tried to convince herself she was in love with, but without success. "I'd like to see you again," he said. "To hear about your family. About you. Don't worry, I quite understand this phone call wasn't because you decided you were wrong about us. I'm not that foolish. Dinner together would be for friendship's sake only. If we met at six o'clock, that would give us plenty of time to talk before I'd need to leave. We could even go Dutch, if that would make dining together more acceptable to you."

She hesitated. He clearly seemed to understand where she was coming from regarding him. And, she had to admit, after getting the cold shoulder from Paavo, it felt good to talk to someone who actually wanted to be with her. But still...

On the other hand, if she didn't go, she would sit here in her apartment hoping Paavo would drop by or call. How pathetic!

But then, dinner at six meant she could leave her apartment a little after five-thirty, and be home a little after eight in case Paavo *did* find time to call or visit.

"All right," she said. The best spot for them to meet would be a restaurant that was basic, without any of the ambiance that might give Derrick the wrong impression. "I know just the place."

5

The next morning, Paavo and Yosh entered Bert Lambert's home. It was a modest place just off of Lake Street in the city's inner Richmond district, a neighborhood of single houses and two-story flats surrounding shop-lined Clement and Geary streets. It was a brownstone with white trim, grilled windows, and an overhang at the entry protected the two detectives from the rain that had returned.

Paavo knocked, both as a courtesy and a caution. Sometimes people the police thought lived alone, didn't. And at times, those closest to the victim were the least happy to have homicide inspectors come to call.

No one answered.

Yosh held a penlight on the lock as Paavo used a curved tension hook and sawtooth comb to pick it. A couple of minutes later, it clicked open.

"Will you look at this place?" Yosh exclaimed as the two men stepped into a large, sparsely furnished room. White rugs lay on glistening golden oak hardwood, and bright, abstract oils hung on stark white walls. Yosh stopped and peered down reflexively at his loafers, then up at Paavo. Paavo shrugged. Lambert wouldn't care about dirt in his house anymore.

The old house had had the guts torn out of it, Paavo thought, then winced at the involuntary memory that caused of Lambert's corpse. The remodeling had removed the walls separating the living room, dining room and kitchen. A teak dining table and a white and black marble kitchen counter marked the different living areas.

Paavo gave the house a once over, glancing into the bedroom with a king-size bed, the bathroom, and two closets. The house had all the homeyness and personal warmth of a spread in *Architectural Digest*. Not a washcloth out of place.

"I'll take the kitchen," Yosh said. "I want to see what this guy used to eat. What in the world could he find that wasn't messy? I'll bet you he's got hand-painted, exotic plates and glasses in the kitchen. Not anything anyone uses. Maybe fancy European pots and pans, too. Just like someone we know, right, pal?"

"I'll start in the bedroom," Paavo said, ignoring what he knew to be a jab at Angie's money and possessions. Joking about Angie's money was a favorite homicide pastime. He didn't find it funny.

He continued on with his inspection. He wasn't looking for anything specific, but for something that felt out of place, off beat, or somehow significant to the mystery of Bertram Lambert's death. He began with the bureau, pulling out drawers, one by one, going through socks and underwear. Most drawers were empty. The walk-in closet had one suit, two sports coats, slacks, shirts, sweaters, shoes and ties, all arranged by style, then color. In the back was a clothes hamper. He opened it. A shirt, boxers, tee shirt and one pair of socks, all folded, lay in the bottom. Who in the world folded dirty clothes? The guy had been beyond anal.

A shoebox of photos sat on a shelf. Paavo flipped through

them. They were all old. One, in particular, caught his eye. A young unsmiling Bertram stared at the camera while his older sister gripped his hand and frowned, as if she were already displeased with him. He put the shoebox up on the shelf once more.

He saved the desk for last. It was a Scandinavian teak with only a single drawer below the desktop. Lambert obviously wasn't one to fill his home with clutter.

Under the desk was a wastebasket. Paavo picked it up. He didn't need to overturn it because it only had three pieces of paper. A PG&E bill, a Macy's bill, and a flyer that said "Roswell: The True Story."

Opening the flyer, he saw it was the story of the alien space ship that was said to have landed in Roswell, New Mexico in the summer of 1947. He was familiar with the tale. Maybe Lambert was as well, and that's why he had thrown it away. The Macy's bill showed Lambert had recently bought a two-hundred-dollar pair of shoes on sale, and the PG&E bill was unremarkable. Paavo dropped everything back into the trash.

He scrutinized the room once more. Unless Lambert's murder was strictly a random act, the reason he was killed had to be found through a careful study of his life—his job, his home, his hobbies. The answer was very likely somewhere in this meticulously tidy home, and Paavo intended to find it. Slowly and methodically, he went through Lambert's personal papers, address books, day planners, and the few scraps of loose paper he could find.

He found the names of very few people, men or women, who might have been friends. It seemed that, whatever Lambert's hopes had been in coming to San Francisco, they hadn't been met.

Back in Homicide, Paavo found himself frustrated by the complete lack of evidence at the crime scene and everywhere else they had looked. Uniformed officers were once more canvassing the neighbors, but so far nothing new had turned up.

Paavo had walked so many circles around his desk that Yosh had finally told him to get away for a while, to take a break. And, adding to Paavo's general state of irritation was that he couldn't get Angie's phone message out of his mind. He should have just called her back yesterday, said, "All's well," and hung up.

But he hadn't. And he couldn't.

She had mentioned a new business to him. Images of her excitement about it came to mind. She was probably bursting with news. The only decent thing would be to hear about it in person. After all, they had been so close, quite close, not long ago. To see her about this was only right.

Finally, convinced, at five forty-five, he rode the elevator up to Angie's twelfth-floor apartment and knocked on her door. After waiting a few minutes, he knocked again. Seeing her always helped him remember there's more to life than the stench of a horrible way to die and autopsies.

Sometimes, like now, he needed that remembrance.

Stanfield Bonnette opened the apartment door across the hall. "She's not home."

Paavo had never cared for Angie's neighbor. Angie thought it was jealousy, but it was simple dislike. The man relished being the bearer of bad, or at least irritating, news. "Did she give you any idea when she might return?" Paavo asked.

"Oh, it'll be late." Stan folded his skinny arms. "Quite late, I'd imagine," he added with measured insouciance.

Paavo waited, one eyebrow slightly arched. It was obvious Bonnette was dying to tell everything he knew.

"She's gone out with an old boyfriend," Bonnette said, scarcely able to prevent a smile from forming on his lips. "A very close old boyfriend. An astrophysicist, in fact. My suggestion is," he delicately coughed as he was shutting his door, "don't wait up for her."

The Wings of an Angel was a small North Beach restaurant. The owners, Vinnie Freiman, Butch Pagozzi and Earl White, had been lifelong friends and partners. Partners in crime, to be precise, and because of that, cellmates. Now in their sixties, after their last caper was derailed by Paavo, they decided to go straight. With Angie's help, they learned to run a restaurant and made it a favorite among people who lived in the city and wanted tasty, inexpensive Italian food.

Angie stepped inside the restaurant, pulling the door shut behind her.

"'Ey, Miss Angie, good ta see ya." Earl, who had the build of a fire hydrant, greeted her warmly in his role as maître d', waiter, and busboy. Butch cooked, and no one knew what Vinnie did, except that he handled the money and kept Butch and Earl in line.

"Hi, Earl," Angie said as she searched the small restaurant. Despite telling herself that this meeting was strictly business, she'd taken great care with her outfit, settling on a pale blue Donna Karan suit and sapphire earrings. To her surprise, she found that she had butterflies in her stomach. "I'm going to be eating with a fr—" There he was. She stopped speaking. He waved, smiling broadly. Just like in the old days.

He was still the good-looking man she remembered. His hair was light brown and wiry with streaks of gray, although he was only in his mid-thirties. His complexion was slightly ruddy, his eyes hazel, his lips wide, and his front teeth had a boyish space between them that gave a devil-may-care look to the serious astrophysicist that he was. She smiled back.

"Do you know dat guy, Miss Angie?" Earl asked suspiciously. "Or am I gonna hafta teach him some manners?"

"He's the old friend I'm here to meet." She walked toward Derrick, who stood up as she neared. Earl grabbed a couple of menus and hurried after her.

"Angelina." Derrick grabbed her outstretched hand. Instead of shaking it as she'd intended, he pulled her close and kissed her cheek, then smiled at her. He was a bit under six feet tall with a sinewy build. "Even more beautiful than I remember."

"Hello, Derrick," she replied. The familiar scent of his cologne, Ralph Lauren's Polo, brought back memories of nightclubs and dances they'd gone to, and the way he'd held her close. He was dressed in the casual style she remembered him favoring, an off-white oxford shirt, unbuttoned at the top, no tie, a taupe tweed sports coat, dark gray slacks, and black-tasseled loafers.

"Miss Angie," Earl said, at her elbow. "Do you wanna sit down?"

"Oh." She turned to see him holding the chair out. "Thanks." Pulling her hand from Derrick's grasp, she sat.

Derrick was about to move his chair catty-corner to hers rather than facing her, when Earl quickly stepped between them, forcing Derrick to stay where he was. "We got some specials today."

Angie gawked at him.

"We got spaghetti an' meatballs, polenta an' sausage, an' meatball sangwiches."

Considering that those were the usual offerings, she gave Earl a cold stare.

"You're the culinary expert, Angelina," Derrick said with enthusiasm. "I defer to your judgment."

Earl's eyebrows shot up high as his head swiveled toward Derrick.

Angie sat a little taller. "The spaghetti and meatballs for Mr. Holton, Earl, and the polenta for me."

"Got it. Wine?"

"House red is fine."

"Anyt'ing else?"

"That's it," she said giving him a nod that clearly said, "Get lost."

Glancing from her to Derrick, he frowned, then said ominously, "I'll be back."

The minute Earl left, Derrick leaned toward her. "How have you been?"

"Fine. Quite fine, in fact." Small talk wasn't what she was here for. She folded her hands. "The reason I called was to talk to you about UFOs." She quickly told him about her Fantasy Dinners business and apologized for asking a serious scientist about such a subject.

"Your own business!" Derrick beamed at her. "How very impressive! Well, I can certainly tell you about UFOs. There's much to tell." Their eyes met, and he stopped talking. Her discomfort grew as his gaze seemed to take in her every feature, her earrings, her hair, and then settled on her lips. "I'm sorry, Angie." He reached across the table and took her hand in his. "I know I promised not to think about the past, but seeing you again—"

"'Scuze me," Earl said gruffly, arriving with a carafe of wine and their glasses. "'Ere's your wine. You want I should pour it, Miss Angie?" While Earl spoke, he stared hard at Derrick, until he let go of Angie's hand and leaned back in his chair to wait until Earl finished his task.

At Angie's nod, Earl poured them each a glass then, with another deadly glance at Derrick, put the carafe down on the table with a thud and left.

Derrick bent toward Angie. "I get the feeling he disapproves of me for some reason."

"Don't worry," she said. "He's that way with everyone. So, what can you tell me about UFO's?"

Before replying, Derrick gave a nervous glance toward the swinging doors to the kitchen where Earl had gone. "It's funny you should ask, because that's what I'm going to hear about this evening. I want to learn all I can about the most extraordinary age our world has ever known. Even our government is finally acknowledging that something strange is going on. To think, it's happening right now. Right here—"

"Sorry." Earl put their salads in front of them, plus a basket of sourdough bread and butter.

"Thank you," Derrick said through clenched teeth.

"Yeah." Earl left.

Derrick looked at her. "Angie, before we talk about all that, I want to know about you. You haven't married I take it. Are you engaged?"

"I haven't married, and I'm not engaged, although I'm... I'm quite serious about someone."

"There's still some hope for me, then." He smiled as broadly and easily as ever.

She had to set him straight. "I don't—"

"Don't answer! Give me time." He winked mischievously, his eyes sparkling. Yes, he was definitely still handsome. But still not her type. Was it possible for a man to be too fawning? Too smiley? She wouldn't have thought so, but what else could she have objected to about him? Paavo didn't have a fawning bone in his entire six-foot-two-inch body.

On the other hand, Connie could use someone who would fawn over her. Since her divorce, she hadn't found a man she hit it off with. She'd recently dated Angie's cousin, Buddy, an old high school flame, but they both soon realized the flame had died.

The more Angie thought about Connie and Derrick, the more she liked the idea.

"Talk to me about UFO's," she said. Taking a bite of her salad, ostensibly waiting for him to speak, she let her mind spin ways to bring Derrick and Connie together.

"I promised, didn't I?" He gave a soft laugh and reached out, clearly planning to take hold of her left hand, since she was holding a salad fork in her right one.

"I know Miss Angie likes ta eat her salad wit' her dinner," Earl said, balancing a tray that was tottering dangerously close to Derrick's left ear. "So I brung it out ta you fast. I done good, right, Miss Angie?"

Derrick pulled back his hand and leaned away from Earl's perilous tray.

Angie smoothed the napkin over her lap. "You did good, Earl."

He placed the food in front of them. "Anyt'ing else?"

"We're fine," Derrick said, a little too forcefully. Earl frowned and walked away.

"As you were saying about the UFOs," Angie coaxed.

"Oh ... yes." Derrick sipped some wine, then took a taste of his spaghetti and meatballs, and nodded appreciatively. "The help here might not be the best, but this tastes great."

Angie just smiled.

"Anyway," Derrick began, "ufologists believe that from the beginning of recorded time man has known he wasn't alone in the universe. In fact, they say there's good evidence we came here from somewhere else. That's the real reason there's no scientific proof that Darwin was right, no missing link to prove that man evolved from other animals. It's not because God created man, but because man came from another planet!"

Whoa. "That's wild," she said.

"Ufologists point to very convincing evidence. They believe humans look to the stars because we're searching for our home.

And that someday, soon, our ancestors will come back to earth for us. All the ancient prophecies talk of it, the most famous being Nostradamus."

The origin of mankind and ancient prophesies were not at all what she was expecting to hear from Derrick. What she'd hoped for were tales of little green men and flying saucers. "How interesting," she said weakly. "So tell me, do aliens look like us? Do they eat the way we do?"

He frowned, then shrugged as if he didn't know and didn't particularly care. "I've never heard any talk about them eating, although they must. We've evolved differently from them. They're thinner, smaller, with huge black eyes and gray skin. We're far more interesting looking and acting. They're quite curious about our sexuality, you know."

"Oh?" She found herself leaning away from him. He didn't seem to be joking.

He bent closer to her, lowering his voice. "In fact, the prime reason that EBEs—extraterrestrial biological entities—come to earth and abduct humans to is study our reproductive organs and—"

"Derrick! Give me a break. You sound as if you're speaking from experience." Angie grinned as she said this, hoping he would join in.

"Oh, well, I wouldn't want to give that impression." He made a weird chuckle.

Although Derrick had begun by stating what ufologists believed, he had clearly slid into his own belief system. Maybe he wouldn't be as right for Connie as she'd imagined? But then, she'd dated him, even brought him home to meet her family. He was a good and brilliant scientist, not a UFO nut. "We both know the people who go on TV or write books about being abducted are making up stories to get money. It's all a hoax."

His eyes darted, almost as if he was looking for one of the aliens to be watching them. "I wouldn't be too sure of that if I were you," he whispered, then gave her a knowing glance. "It could well be true. Science now shows that there's life beyond Mars."

"Life beyond Mars? Isn't that the name of a book coming out soon by Algernon?"

Derrick stopped twirling spaghetti onto his fork in mid-twirl. "Algernon!" his voice boomed with disgust. "You're joking, right? You can't be saying that guy's name seriously!"

Angie tried to ignore the way the other diners suddenly turned and stared at them. Even Earl stuck his head out of the kitchen and frowned. What was going on with Derrick?

Derrick's voice dropped. "Algernon doesn't have any idea what he's talking about. The man's a fraud."

"A fraud?" Eyes wide, her thoughts turned to Triana Crisswell, rich and overly impressionable. Although she had suspected Triana might well be the victim of some con artists, it was disconcerting to hear her suspicion confirmed this way. "How do you know?"

"The people I read and the lectures I go to have proved it. Later this evening, the lecture I told you I'll be attending is by a speaker who knows all about EBEs." He began eating again.

A thought sprang to mind. She needed to learn more about EBEs and UFOs, and she knew Connie wasn't doing anything that night. She should have Connie join her at the lecture and then introduce her to Derrick. A wealthy onetime NASA scientist might be just the thing to bring Connie cheer, as long as he could get over this strange idea that EBEs might really exist. He was quite normal just five years ago, so maybe he was going through a weird phase. "Maybe I should go to his talk tonight, too," she mused. "It might help me with my business."

"Great! I'll take you. You'll enjoy meeting my friends. We'll help you forget all about that charlatan, Algernon."

"Speaking of friends, I'm supposed to meet one—"

"The one you're serious about?" he asked.

She smiled. "No. A woman. A girlfriend."

He smiled back. "In that case, the more the merrier. The meeting is in Tardis Hall."

"I've never heard of it."

"It's a converted warehouse at the foot of Brannan, near the Embarcadero. They'll be destroying it soon as part of the rebuilding of the waterfront area. So we've cordoned off a part of it, and for a tiny fee, the City—now its owners—lets us use it."

Earl walked up to them and slapped the bill on the table. "You finished? I guess you gotta get goin'. You gonna see *him* tonight, Miss Angie?"

"Not very soon, I'm afraid," Angie said, understanding exactly who Earl was referring to.

"Is he woikin'?"

"As usual." She wished he were the one with her right now.

Earl looked at his watch. "Maybe he'll get off woik sooner den you t'ought?"

"No. He never does," she said with dejection.

Derrick picked up the bill and began to look it over.

Earl snatched it out of Derrick's hand. "In dat case, why don' you two guys stay here and have some dessert? You two don' wanna go off alone nowhere, not jus' da two a you. We got some good pie-alla-uh, you know, wit' ice cream on it. Stay. Kick back. Take your shoes off."

Derrick glanced at his watch. "I'm afraid it's time for us to leave," he said, lifting the bill from Earl's fingers.

"No need. It's oily." He grabbed the bill again.

"Oily?" Derrick glanced from the bill to his fingers.

"Early." Angie translated.

Derrick lunged for the bill.

Earl swung his arm behind his back and jumped out of the way. "How 'bout some coffee? But no more wine, t'ough." With his free hand he yanked the carafe off the table and retreated another step. "I don' wan' Miss Angie ta lose her good sense. Wha' *little* of it she's got left."

"Just the bill, Earl," Angie said sternly.

"Da bill. You sure you know wha' you're doin'?"

She nodded.

"Don' say I didn' warn you."

6

After leaving The Wings of an Angel restaurant, Angie got into her car, grabbed her cell phone and made a call. Not until she mentioned that Derrick Holton was smart, handsome, with a good job, and single, did Connie agree to meet her at Tardis Hall.

As Angie drove toward the Hall, she had to admit to being curious as to why a onetime NASA scientist had left his job and was now teaching and interested in extraterrestrials. It seemed a strange career move.

The city's weather continued to be foggy and overcast, and its recent showers caused her tires to squeal on the rain-soaked pavement as she pulled into the parking lot. Before shutting off the engine, Angie ran her windshield wipers a couple of times.

Clear windshields didn't improve the looks of Tardis Hall. Over two-stories tall, it was boxy and warehouse-like, with few windows. Although the entrance was well lit, the rest of the building looked dirty and uninviting.

She texted Connie and told her where she was parked, although not a lot of cars were in the lot, and Ferrari Portofino's tended to stand out.

Before long, Connie's small gray Toyota pulled in beside her.

"I wonder if I'm overdressed for a lecture?" Connie said as they met outside their cars to walk to the Tardis entrance. "I kept thinking about how great you described this guy, and might have gotten a bit carried away." Under a heavy coat, she was wearing a Kelly-green cocktail dress with a plunging neckline. Connie's full figure was buxom enough to carry it off.

"If you'd like Derrick to notice you," Angie said, "once you take that coat off, he definitely will. Anyway, I told you he seems lonely. I think he could use someone down-to-earth to spend time with him."

As they walked toward the entrance to the Hall, they saw that a small line had formed to buy tickets. "This event looks popular, kind of," Connie muttered.

"I'm sure a lot of people will show up at the last minute," Angie said.

Angie was about to say more, when a stout man sitting at a small folding table caught her attention. Brochures were stacked on it, plus a sign that read:

New members! Free drawings.
$100 to the lucky winner! Join today!

The man at the table stood as they neared. He had a round belly, thinning brown hair and a tiny, Hitler-shaped mustache. He thrust a brochure toward them. The title intrigued her. "Roswell: The True Story."

She was about to reach for the brochure when she then saw Derrick waving at them. She took Connie's arm, and they hurried to reach him. He tried to put his arm around Angie, but she stepped to the side. "Derrick, I'd like you to meet my good friend, Connie Rogers. Connie, this is Derrick Holton."

Derrick held out his hand and said it was nice to meet her.

Connie took a moment before she placed hers in his and, with a look of sheer bliss, she checked him out from his neatly trimmed brown hair to his tasseled loafers, then murmured something that sounded a bit like, "Same here."

"The doors should be opening anytime now. Here are two tickets for you. No need to wait in line." Derrick clapped his hands together and rocked onto his toes as he excitedly scanned the area. "Please excuse me for now. I've been given the honor of introducing tonight's speaker, and I need to check on things backstage. But if you're free after the lecture, I'd love to take both of you out for a drink. How would that be?"

Angie turned to Connie who nodded enthusiastically. "That would be quite nice," she said.

"I knew you'd agree." Derrick said, smiling into Angie's eyes. A blond, pony-tailed man wearing a faded plaid shirt and loose, dirty jeans came up to them. He wore thick wire-rimmed glasses. "Ah! Here's my friend, Sir Galahad. He'll take care of you."

Angie and Connie shook his hand as Derrick introduced them.

"Twill be an honor most joyous, m'ladies," Galahad said.

Angie chuckled and expected Derrick to laugh or somehow react to Galahad's bizarre way of speaking. Derrick didn't bat an eyelash and disappeared into the crowd. Galahad gave Angie a big smile. His teeth were as gnarled as his speech.

"So, doth m'ladies share Sir Holton's interest in things skyward?" he asked, pointing upward.

What was with this guy? "Not exactly," Angie said. "This is our first time here."

Galahad led them into the stark entry hall. The walls were a grimy yellow color and streaked with fingerprints. The gray linoleum floor was even more worn and dirty. Facing them was a wall of unfinished plywood with double doors in the middle. Angie assumed they led to the auditorium.

Hanging by the doors was a poster of a man who looked like the reincarnation of a frizzle-haired Albert Einstein, and equally old. Across the top of the poster, written with a red felt-marker, were the words: DR. FREDERICK MOSSHAD—HERE TONIGHT!!!

"Ah! 'Tis well-chosen that you come this eve. A fine presentation we shall hear. The learned Dr. Mosshad will speak of what the astronauts on the space station really saw." His voice dropped to a whisper and he pushed his glasses back up to the bridge of his nose. "The classified material they have been so ignobly forced to keep secret."

"They've kept secrets?" Angie thought the whole purpose of space flights and stations was to collect data, not to hide it.

"Of course they've kept secrets, m'lady! All the astronauts have. Did you not know that?" He gaped at her as if she were the odd one of the two. "The hair on your head would stand on end if you heard what they have seen."

Once more, she found herself wondering if Galahad was serious or if this was all one big cosmic joke.

"Someday the government will be forced to give up its secrets. Then 'twill be as all the demons of hell were loosed upon the land. Do you not agree?"

Angie faced Connie. "Could be," Connie muttered, looking equally confused.

His eyes shifted from side to side. "That means you two are smarter than most in this land. Therefore, you must beware. Too many people believe they have all the answers, but they know not!"

"Well, forsooth!" Angie said. Wait until she got her hands on Derrick for leaving her with this bozo. "If you'll excuse us, I think we'll go find the ladies' room."

He gave them a quick nod. "I beg your indulgence as well. Sir Derrick forgot, as is his wont, that I must go set up the projector. Dr. Mosshad will require it."

Galahad pushed his glasses high on his nose again and marched off.

"Nice meeting you," she murmured. Real nice. About as nice as getting a tetanus shot.

She and Connie saw that the double doors were now open and people were going into the small auditorium area. Folding chairs had been set up in rows facing a podium, and the expanse behind it was covered in heavy, dark red drapery.

They found seats in the middle of a row near the front of the auditorium. Connie went in first, wanting a place she could clearly see Derrick. She excitedly told Angie she found him to be both handsome and interesting.

The two no sooner sat down when a small, gaunt man wearing a black jacket, black turtleneck and black slacks gave a jaunty nod of the head and took the chair right next to Angie.

"Hello, lovely lady," he said.

She could scarcely see his face under a thick head of steel gray hair so long and thick it nearly reached the equally thick eyebrows that shadowed his eyes. His thin, purple-hued mouth peeked out from a bushy beard and mustache. Was the entire hall filled with nothing but oddballs? There were plenty of empty seats in the hall, so why did this guy sit right next to her?

"Good evening," she said, then turned away.

"Is this your first time at a NAUTS event?" His high-pitched voice had an excited, animated quality.

His words caught her attention. "Naughts? As in zeros?"

He chuckled. "Not exactly. It stands for the National Association of Ufological Technology Scientists. And it's a play on *astro*-NAUTS."

"Ah. I didn't know that was the name of the sponsoring group. It's my first time here."

"So nice to have you." He clasped his hands, much like a teacher about to give a presentation. Or, considering how bushy-bearded, black clad, and gaunt he was, a preacher of some back-to-basics-and-not-much-food religious cult. "They're a fairly new group—a splinter group—seeking the truth."

"A splinter of what?" Angie asked.

"It was quite distasteful," the stranger said, dropping his voice and shifting closer. "Originally, there was only the Prometheus Group. It was made up of those members who considered themselves to have a scientific bent. It was run by a genius named Igor Mikhailovich Neumann. But ten years ago, Neumann died. After that, the Prometheans began to move into the paranormal. That caused the true scientists to leave and form the NAUTS. The two groups now hate each other."

"Really?" It was odd that Derrick hadn't mentioned anything to her about the NAUTS or the Prometheans. But since there was bad blood between the two groups, that explained why Derrick had grown so heated about Algernon. "I've heard of the Prometheus Group and Algernon," she said, thinking of her Fantasy Dinner for Triana Crisswell.

"Algernon ... yes." A mysterious half-smile touched the gaunt man's lips. "Have you met Algernon?"

"Not yet. I hope to soon."

He nodded. "Well, Algernon leads one sect and tonight's speaker, Dr. Mosshad, founded the other."

"Sect? You make it sound like a religion."

He smiled. "It is, rather. Sort of like the Protestants and the Catholics. Variations on the same theme, each believing they alone hold the true Truth. Perhaps because so many people these days refuse to believe in God, they now search for other things to believe in. My name is Malachi, by the way," the gaunt man said. "And you are?"

"I'm Angie." She didn't give her last name since her nerves were growing increasingly edgy about being here. She didn't know if it was because Derrick had abandoned them, or this strange man. She turned her head. The chairs were filling up with people with several standing on the periphery. But then, she noticed a tall, muscular fellow who stood alone with his back to the wall. He wore black sunglasses and a black suit, and his head was turned in her direction, as if he were watching her or Connie or Malachi.

The last thing he needed in this hall were those sunglasses, but because of them, she couldn't tell who he was eyeing. When she stared back at him, however, he abruptly turned his head away.

Science fiction stories about 'Men in Black' came to mind. Suddenly, she felt surrounded by all kinds of other-worldly weirdness.

That did it. She and Connie needed to get out of here. The clock near the stage showed nine o'clock. She checked her watch. Yes, the time was right. Her hopes for seeing or talking to Paavo tonight had been dashed, but he probably hadn't shown up, anyway.

She mentally kicked herself for still caring.

Angie then turned to Connie. But Connie was watching Derrick at the side of the podium talking to some people. If eyeballs could be glued to someone, Connie's would be attached to Derrick.

"Connie?" she said. "Connie, I'm ready to leave."

"The hall is filling up. I wonder if he's nervous," Connie murmured, then sighed. "He's really good looking!"

Angie gave up and turned again to Malachi. "May I ask you," she said, since the man seemed to know the subject, "if you have ever heard what aliens eat?"

He stared at her blankly for a moment, then his lips curled into a smile and he stroked his chin. "That's a matter of considerable speculation," he replied gravely. "But no definitive answers."

It figures, Angie thought.

"What little we know, we've discovered by hypnotizing

victims of alien abductions. Some people are abducted over and over, and in time, despite their fear, they develop an understanding of what's being done to them."

Alien abductions? "You believe there really are alien abductions?" she asked.

"Of course! In fact, tonight's emcee, Derrick Holton, is quite an expert on the subject."

Angie's eyes widened so far they would have fallen out if not firmly attached to her head. "He is? What does he say happens to the abductees?"

"In most cases, both men and women are stripped, strapped onto a table, and then long needles and probes are stuck into their bodies, eyes, nose, brains, and especially in the, er, gonad area."

Angie gawked at him, taking this in and wondering why Derrick would have become an expert in such nonsense. He was once a brilliant scientist. "It's amazing," she finally replied, amazing that anyone would believe that if there were aliens roaming around the galaxy, they had nothing better do to than to study human sexuality. The idea gave voyeurism a whole new dimension.

Derrick had also mentioned the sexual angle. Was this abduction nonsense just erudite porn for the wigged out? Derrick used to seem so normal.

The small audience of at most fifty people, a few college age, many middle-aged or older, was growing restless. She checked her watch. Although the lights had dimmed, it was now nine-fifteen. The eight-thirty starting time for the lecture must have been MST—Martian Standard Time. It certainly had nothing to do with the Pacific Time the rest of the West Coast used.

She realized Malachi was still talking to her. "... and the government won't admit to any of this because they want to keep it hidden from their enemies..."

Angie desperately hoped Dr. Mosshad would be a lot more interesting than old Malachi was.

Now, even Derrick was gone. Angie leaned closer to Connie and whispered, "This is forty-five minutes late. I think we should just leave."

"But we're supposed to meet Derrick after the lecture for drinks," Connie reminded her. "Give it a few more minutes."

Angie sighed. She should have known bringing Connie here was a mistake.

Just then, Derrick bounded onto the platform that served as a stage and held up his hands to quiet the crowd.

When he had their attention, he said, "Friends, I'm Derrick Holton. I was going to make some opening remarks and give an introduction listing our speaker's many accomplishments, but since we're running late, I'll simply say, here is a man who needs no introduction, Dr. Frederick Mosshad!"

A small, frail-looking old man stepped out from behind a curtain before the podium and paused to thunderous applause as Derrick quickly left the stage.

Mosshad took a step forward when a blinding white light flashed over the entire auditorium. The light was so bright people had to cover their eyes.

They cried out. But then, a painfully high-pitched squeal blared from the speakers around the room. Angie not only squeezed her eyes shut, but needed to press her hands hard against her ears. The light and sound seemed to go on and on, growing more unbearable with each passing second.

But then, as suddenly as it began, the bright light vanished, and the room turned quiet as death.

Angie lifted her head. Mosshad and Derrick were gone from the stage, and the audience members gaped in stunned silence.

"What was that?" Connie whispered to Angie. "What's going on?"

"I don't know," Angie said, and then turned to Malachi. "Do you know what just happened?"

He sat rigidly facing the stage as a buzz of voices began spreading throughout the hall, growing quickly louder. "I must think," he said.

I must leave, she thought. "Let's get out of here, Connie," she said to Connie's agreeing nod. The din in the room grew louder as they picked up their coats and handbags.

"Look at the time!" came a shout from the front.

"The time?" Angie glanced up at the clock to the right of the stage. Nine-thirty, and then at her watch. She tapped it a couple of times. "My watch says nine-twenty. Has it stopped? My two-thousand-dollar unstoppable Movado has stopped? Connie, are you wearing a watch?"

"No, but my phone says nine-twenty."

"My watch stopped, too," Malachi said. Suddenly an expression of a beatific vision came over him. He climbed up on his chair and threw his arms high overhead. In a loud, booming voice he cried, "They're here! The aliens! Look at the clock, then at your watches! Time stopped for us. It was an alien abduction—*of us!*"

First the auditorium seemed to freeze in place, but then a woman screamed. Another fainted.

Angie turned to Malachi. "What's going on!"

Ignoring her, Malachi, still on the chair, shouted at the small crowd, his voice booming. "Where is Dr. Mosshad? He needs to explain this to us!"

A cry rose up from the audience as people began to clamor for Mosshad to tell them what had happened, to assure them that everything was all right, that they would be fine despite the mass abduction many seem to believe had happened.

Mass hysteria, Angie thought, and was about to step past Malachi to get out of there when Connie grabbed her arm.

"Wait! Look. Derrick's back on stage," Connie said. "He'll tell us what's happening."

The audience grew hushed, expectant. People sat and waited, as did Connie. Finally, Angie, too, sat back down, as did Malachi.

"My friends," Derrick began, his voice softer than Angie had ever heard it. "Something happened here tonight. Something extraordinary, perhaps miraculous. There was a light, and a ringing that went on for a long, long while. When it stopped, those of us backstage discovered we all had been given a message—the same message. I can't say we heard it, because we didn't hear it with our ears. We heard it some other way, and it became embedded deep in our brains. I know it's hard to believe, but friends, I will share with you, now, the message we were given."

Derrick drew in a deep breath and looked out over the hall, his gaze meeting those in the audience, one by one.

"We have been told that Dr. Mosshad"—he swallowed hard before continuing—"Dr. Mosshad has been abducted by a life force from another world!"

When Paavo left Homicide late that night after spending more fruitless hours on the mutilation case, all he could think about was Angie dating an old boyfriend. An astrophysicist, no less. That is, if Stan Bonnette's report was true. Stan knew how to aggravate Paavo—he'd done it a number of times.

Paavo drove toward home, but then made a U-turn. He had to know, one way or the other, if she'd already moved on. If she had, then everything his friends and coworkers, who were essentially the same people, said about her was true: that she was a rich dilettante who liked the intrigue and danger of dating a homicide inspector, but as soon as something more exciting came along—like an astrophysicist maybe?—she'd be gone.

And if that was the case, he'd be better off knowing it now and not waste another second thinking about her.

At her apartment, he lightly tapped on her door. He wondered if she might be sleeping... or otherwise engaged, if Stan's story was true. He felt foolish—like a love-sick schoolboy, checking up on the girl of his dreams.

To his relief, she opened the door. He fixed his attention wholly on her, waiting to see if she would invite him in, or if he'd notice the shift of an eye, a flinch, the slightest nuance that might tell him he should in any way give credence to her neighbor's words.

"You're here! Come in," she said. "Oh, my God. It was so exciting! I couldn't believe it. I mean, it was so incredible! How did you find out already? Is it already on the news? Oh, of course! The police band radio."

He stared at her, baffled, even as relief surged through him that she was alone. "Angie, hold on," he said as they moved into her apartment and shut the door. "What did I find out?"

"You mean you haven't heard?" A small furrow formed between her eyebrows.

"I came in answer to your message. To hear about your new business. I'm sorry it's so late, but—"

"It's okay. I was still up. I was out... with Connie."

Their eyes met and held a long moment. He loved the warmth of her eyes, but now he saw something more in them... a shift. "With Connie?" he murmured.

She swallowed and stepped back from him. "Yes. We went to hear a lecture," she said, dropping her gaze to look anywhere but at him. "It was held at a cute, but strange little place called Tardis Hall. I'd never heard of it before..."

"Me, neither," he said, noticing her sudden uneasiness.

"It's at the foot of Brannan, near the water. But anyway, as we waited for the lecture to start, the lecturer was abducted by aliens."

Of all the strange things Angie had ever said to him over the months he'd known her, of all the stories she'd dreamed up, and "little white lies" she'd told him, that one took the cake. "Aliens? What kind of aliens? And who did they abduct?"

"I'm talking about little green men. Or gray. Or whatever color people say they are. But who really knows anyway, right?" She then took a deep breath as if realizing she was babbling. "They abducted our lecturer."

"You're joking." His voice, his words, were flat.

"Well, I'm not saying the roof opened up and Darth Vader grabbed the guy," she explained. "But someone made an announcement telling us that was what happened." She bit her bottom lip and then quickly added, "It was probably a publicity stunt."

"I'd say so."

"You may be right. Let's forget it. Would you like coffee? A beer? Have you eaten?"

He knew her well enough to know when she wasn't being truthful, and she wasn't now. Stan's words kept echoing in his mind. Maybe Stan was right, or maybe something else was going on. He suddenly didn't want to know. "No, thanks. I should be on my way. I've got a strange case to deal with."

Her eyes widened in surprise or dismay—he couldn't tell. Then she nodded, and whispered, "okay."

He walked to the door. "Goodbye, Angie."

She said nothing as he left.

7

Criminologist Ray Faldo reached his gloved hand into the evidence bag and took out the heavy goggles that had been found on Bertram Lambert's body. A few minutes earlier, Faldo had called and asked Paavo to come down to the lab when he had time. Paavo made time right then and Yosh had joined him.

Now, Paavo watched Faldo blow on the goggles to remove a trace of fingerprint powder and then place them on a table in front of the two inspectors. Faldo was a pro. Even though he'd worked in the crime lab over twenty years, he didn't simply put in his hours and go home at the end of the day. He still approached his work ready for the excitement that discovery could bring. For that reason, Paavo had gone to him about the goggles in the first place. "Do more than test for prints," Paavo had said. "Find out what in the hell those goggles are."

"This thing is old," Faldo said as they peered down at the heavy black object. "Seventy, eighty years, at least." He picked up a black lacquer Japanese chopstick and used it as a pointer. "You can tell that from the way it was made, and the way the glass and metal sheathing has become scratched and worn from handling. For the longest time, I had no idea what the goggles were supposed to be used for. I emailed a bunch of colleagues. I got lots of crazy suggestions, but nothing useful. Then, I happened to have them on at the exact right moment."

He picked them up and gave them to Paavo. "Take a look."

Paavo peered through the goggles. The lab looked dark, fuzzy, and distorted. Faldo switched off the light.

"Hey!" Yosh cried. "Why'd you do that? I can't see a thing!"

But Paavo could. "Don't reach out that way, Yosh," he said. "You're about to hit a glass beaker."

"What?" Yosh pulled back his hand. "You can see in the dark with those things?"

Faldo spoke. "That's what I discovered. I was looking through them when the lights flickered. That's when I thought the view had changed, but the flicker was brief, so I turned off the lights in the lab and put the goggles back on. What Paavo sees, is what I saw. They're not anywhere as sophisticated as the night vision glasses the military has now, of course, but an early version of that very technology. Something is strange about them, though."

Paavo took the goggles off and handed them to Yosh.

"Holy!" Yosh cried. "Will you look at that! You know, Paavo, we should use something like this when we travel around at night in the city. Can you imagine? We could see the crooks but they couldn't see us? It'd be great! Maybe I should ask Nancy to get me a pair for my birthday."

Faldo flicked the lights back. "There you have it."

"You said there was something strange about them," Paavo said to Faldo as Yosh took the goggles off and gazed at them admiringly.

"I looked through catalogues and manuals about old military gear—early night goggles and such. The earliest versions were very poor. Huge, bulky things. The current generation of them, issued during the Vietnam war, used a very different technology—they were slimmer, more reliable, easier to use and see with. These seem to be a prototype of that new generation. What's strange is that they've never shown up in a catalogue or anywhere else. I searched everywhere I could think of online once I knew what to look for, but zilch.

"I could find no documented history of the evolution from the earliest ones to the night goggles of today. It's as if the technology to make them was developed overnight—from one lousy version, to the next one that actually worked. These goggles look like the prototype for the current generation—a secret prototype, from all I can tell. But I have no idea where they came from or who made them."

Paavo and Yosh stared at the strange goggles. "Did you find any more prints on them, or anything that might help us find out where they came from?" Yosh asked.

"They've been wiped spotless except for the one Ramsbottom fingerprint of unknown age," Faldo said.

"Still, thanks for all you've found out," Paavo said.

"Thank P.G. and E. They caused the electricity to go haywire and gave me the clue to the goggles. The electric company giveth and the electric company taketh away—too often these days."

Angie waited for her morning coffee to brew. It had taken her forever to fall asleep last night. All she could think about was Paavo and how strangely he had acted toward her. When she opened the door and saw him, she wanted to throw her arms around him, but his expression and stance were so stern, his gaze so cold, she hung back.

She didn't understand why he was being like that. What had she done?

She poured herself a cup of coffee then sat on her sofa and

opened the morning *Chronicle* online. The first story immediately caught her eye:

Lecturer Disappears - Alien Abduction?

Dr. Frederick Mosshad, astronomer, lecturer, and founder of the National Association of Ufological Technology Scientists, was abducted by space aliens last evening, according to a NAUTS spokesman. That message was given to a group of well over a hundred people waiting to hear Mosshad's lecture at Tardis Hall.

Dr. Derrick Holton, former NASA scientist, said the attendees reported seeing a flash of light and hearing a strange sound fill the auditorium just before the lecturer's disappearance. Such abductions are common, Holton stated, but are rarely so public.

The police have not been asked to investigate. "This isn't a police matter," Holton said. He added that the faithful will gather again at Tardis Hall in two nights to see if Mosshad returns.

Angie stared at the article. If this was a plan for publicity—which she more and more believed, especially when she discovered her watch had not lost any time at all—it had worked very well. She wondered how many more people would show up at Tardis Hall for the next lecture. Maybe she should hire Derrick to do PR for her Fantasy Dinner business? It certainly needed a shot in the arm.

Just like her love life. Quickly, she pushed thoughts of Paavo aside. They hurt too much.

She switched over to her e-mail, hoping against hope that a potential customer might have contacted her about a fantasy dinner through her fantasydinnersare.us website. It would be nice to know at least one other person in the world wanted to cater a fun dinner party.

But the fantasydinnersare.us email was empty. Not even a lousy piece of spam. So much for potential clients beating a path to her door, or her computer.

Just then, her telephone rang. Her first thought was it could be Paavo calling to explain why he was in such a bad mood last night. Maybe to apologize and say he'd come back to see her tonight.

Her hopes fell when she saw the name on the screen as she tapped the Accept button.

"This is Triana Crisswell," the woman said in response to Angie's cheerful hello.

"Mrs. Crisswell, I was just thinking about you," Angie said.

"Good, because I got to tell you, sweetie, you need an idea that's a lollapalooza. This party is simply taking off!"

"What do you mean?" Angie asked.

"I mean the abduction!" She squealed so loudly Angie had to hold the phone away from her ear. "Didn't you hear about it? It's the talk of the whole city."

"I was there," Angie said.

"You *saw* it? Oh, my God! I can't believe it. I hate you! You're soooo lucky!" Triana lowered her voice when she said, "You must realize what this means, sweetie."

"No. I'm afraid I don't," Angie said, increasingly confused.

"It means this party will be so hot, I can't tell you!" Triana shouted. "Already I'm getting calls from people who just have to be included. Like, we're going to have at least two hundred people! Maybe more. I can't fit them all at my house. And, I don't want to wait a whole month. We've got to put on the party now. Immediately."

Now Angie was the one shouting into the phone. "That's impossible. There's too much to do, to plan!"

There was a pause. "A week from Friday, then."

"That still doesn't give me enough time," Angie wailed. "I need a theme, caterers, special decorations. These are supposed to be fantasy dinners, after all."

"Fantasy, shmantasy. Forget the dinner. All I want is a party, right away, with something to munch on. Heck, I don't care if you serve them hotdogs!"

"We need to talk about this," Angie said, desperately attempting to calm her first, and maybe her last, client. "Keep in mind that the best caterers will be booked for next week. Maybe even the ones who aren't the best. Also, to cook for two hundred people, even if it is just hors d'oeuvres, isn't easy. And you do want the best, don't you?"

"Honey." Triana sounded even more annoyed. "You think this is about food? It's about publicity. And it's about making a great name for Algernon. We won't have his books available but we'll pre-sell them, and tell people they'll get autographed copies as soon as the book is published."

"Plus, I haven't even met Algernon. And we haven't agreed on the theme or food or... or anything!"

"I suppose you have a point," Triana said, her tone suddenly hard as chipped ice. "He'll be at a meeting of the Prometheus Group tomorrow. Come to it. I'll text you the address."

Angie sighed. If Triana didn't care about the tastiness of the food or the imaginativeness of the fantasy, why should she? Except that this was her first fantasy dinner, and she had hoped to use it to build her reputation. But she was a clever person, and if this is what her client wanted, she would find a way to deliver it. "Thank you, Mrs. Crisswell. I'll see you tomorrow. Tell me, since the dinner is now too big for your home, where will it be held?"

"There's only one place. Tardis Hall, of course."

8

That afternoon, after another fruitless morning talking to people who knew Bertram Lambert and trying to find any hint as to why he might have been murdered, Paavo returned to his desk.

The first thing he did was to check his voicemail, hoping to hear from Angie telling him what was really going on with her. Maybe even to apologize for lying to him last night.

But there was no message.

He found the official write-up of Lambert's autopsy on his desk. Lambert had been "officially" killed by hammer blows to the head. He was dead when his body was desecrated.

"I've never seen anything like it," Paavo said when he finished reading the autopsy.

"It's crazy." Yosh rolled his chair away from his desk and turned toward Paavo. He had already read the report. "There's not a drop of blood left in the guy's body, his wounds were made with a fine cutting instrument and they'd been cauterized. Who does such a thing? And why?"

"The crime lab suggests some kind of laser was used," Paavo said.

"Who'd get access to lasers like that? Aren't they used for medical procedures and are super expensive?" Yosh cried in frustration. "And why bother? The guy was dead. What was the killer trying to prove?"

Just then, Lt. Hollins, head of the Homicide Bureau, stepped into the big room where the inspectors had their desks. All talking stopped. His face seemed even more lined with worry than usual. "Paavo, Yosh, come into my office."

The lieutenant was in his early fifties, with thinning gray hair and a thickening waistline. He'd been a cop for over twenty years, starting as a beat patrolman at Central Station in North Beach. His dream had been to become the head of Homicide, and five years ago he'd made it. He'd been nursing an ulcer ever since. Even though his job had become, for the most part, administrative instead of investigative, he still had a nose for crime scenes and knew how to follow up on a good lead.

As they entered his office, he walked to the windows and stood in front of them, one hand rubbing the back of his neck.

"Hey there, Chief," Yosh said exuberantly. "Why the long face?"

"Sit down," Hollins said, his voice grim.

They sat. Yosh clamped his mouth shut.

Hollins drew a deep breath. "I just got a call from the Southern station," he said. "There's been another murder. A man, probably in his mid-thirties. It's hard to tell exactly what was done to him, but it sounded a lot like the Stern Grove victim. Our boy—or whoever's responsible for this—is at it again."

Hollins paused, then stared them both in the eyes. "You two need to get out there right now and take over. Keep it quiet. I don't want the press involved. We managed to keep any details of the first mutilation out of the newspapers. If the press gets wind of this second one, it could throw this city into a panic.

Especially with all the kooks already running around sure the world is coming to an end."

The two inspectors stood up. "Where are we going?" Yosh asked.

"The Giants' ballpark. The groundkeepers found him. Right behind second base."

When Angie learned a science fiction and fantasy convention had been taking place the past few days at the Moscone Center, she convinced Connie to attend with her. As they approached the building, they saw two men with gray bodies, huge heads with bulging almond-shaped black eyes, and three fingers on each hand standing in front of the building, smoking cigarettes.

Ah, yes. The no-public-indoor-smoking even applied to beings from outer space. Not far from the entrance, Angie saw a table just like the one that had stood outside Tardis Hall the night before with the same heavyset man with a stubby Hitler-like mustache hawking free drawings for one hundred dollar prizes. Going over to get a brochure crossed her mind, but he was busy talking to several young men, and she was more interested in what was happening inside the convention center.

She and Connie headed past the smokers and bought tickets to enter.

The aliens they had seen outside were dull compared to the costumes inside. Sorcerers, hobbits, and Game of Thrones characters made up the bulk of the fantasy side of the 'con, while the science fiction crowd saw fleets of Martians, Klingons, Luke Skywalkers, Yodas, Mr. Spocks, and Avengers, as well as a number of men in strangely colorful suits carrying miniature old-fashioned telephone booths. She had no idea what that was all about.

"Who are you?" she asked one of them.

"Exactly! Yes, I am!" he cried. His hair was thick and curly.

She stared at him as if he truly was from another planet. "What?" she stammered.

"Not what, who! Dr. Who, I should say!" He giggled. "I love doing that. Just like the old 'Who's on First?' routine. Are you saying you really don't know me?"

She rubbed her forehead, were confused than ever. "I'm afraid I don't"

"I'm a time lord. When not on the BBC I travel through time and space in my tardis."

"Your tardis? What's a tardis?" Angie thought Tardis Hall was named after someone—some wealthy Mr. Tardis. She had no idea it was something a British television time lord used.

"This is a miniature version." He held up the phone booth. "Although it looks like a simple old-fashioned phone box, in fact, when you go inside it turns into my spaceship."

"Uh... right." Angie backed away. "Thank you." She'd just found out more than she ever wanted to know about British sci-fi.

Angie pulled Connie toward the National Association of Ufological Technology Scientists' booth. "Hi," she said to the serious young man behind the booth. He was dressed like a college prep student—white shirt, red tie, no jacket, short, neatly trimmed reddish-brown hair, and a plain, nondescript face. He didn't fit in with this weird crowd at all. It was embarrassing to ask someone so normal looking her question. "Excuse me. Can you tell me a bit about UFOs?" she asked.

"Why, most certainly, ma'am, my pleasure." He had a thick southern accent, and he kept giving her strange looks. "Say, didn't I see you at Tardis Hall the other night?"

Angie was surprised she was so recognizable. "Yes. I was there the night of the abduction."

His smile disappeared. "Oh, I know what night it was, that's for sure. My name's Elvis, by the way."

Of course it is! Angie thought, as she and Connie took a step backwards.

"Don't worry," he said with a long-suffering sigh. "I'm not crazy, my Mama was. She was a big Elvis fan."

Angie and Connie's eyes met, both dubious.

"You asked about UFOs." He picked up a large book from the display in front of him. "Here's a book with photos of them taken all over the U.S. It's on special today. Only $29.95. It's usually ten dollars more."

She glanced at the book he'd stuck in her hands. It was filled with pictures of small shiny objects in the sky. She put it back on the counter. "I don't mean UFOs as such—I mean, what makes them interesting? What real, tangible things come to mind when do you think about UFOs?"

"For starters, Roswell."

"What's Roswell all about?" Angie asked. "I didn't pick up the brochure yet."

He looked at her with amazement. "You mean you really don't know?"

"No."

His mouth dropped open, and he looked at her as if she might be the extra-terrestrial here. "But everybody knows about Roswell."

She was so stunned by the man's reaction to her ignorance, it took her a moment to realize that the shaking she was feeling wasn't the ground moving, but Connie yanking on her arm, trying to get her attention. She left the Roswell devotee and walked off with Connie. "So, what's up?" she asked.

"Look at the picture of the president of this group," Connie whispered. "Did you know that about him?"

Angie took the flyer Connie was holding. Smiling up at her as president of the NAUTS was Derrick Holton. Why hadn't he told her he was president? Was there some reason for keeping it secret?

"I had no idea," she said, as she then looked back at Elvis. "This is too weird. Let's find the Prometheus Group, if they're here."

The two wandered through the convention hall until Angie spotted the group's booth. Here was her chance to find out something about Algernon's association. When she reached the booth, she saw two men and a woman in their late teens or early twenties.

Angie stepped up to the orange-haired fellow who smiled at her, while Connie hung back and watched warily. "Hello," Angie said. "Is Algernon here today?"

He cocked his head and grinned. "Don't I wish!"

"What about Triana Crisswell?" she asked.

He glanced over at his friends. "Hey, you dudes know Triana Crisswell?" He scratched the chest of his X-Files T-shirt as he waited for their response.

"I've heard her name, but I don't know her." A tall, pudgy young woman, dressed in baggy jeans, a long yellow shirt, and a shorter, bulky Levi's jacket, spoke and chewed gum at the same time. She even snapped it.

The other fellow, who wore a baseball cap on backward and a T-shirt that said The End Is Near, replied, "She's not here."

"Well, duhhhh," the girl said, rolling her eyes. "That's pretty obvious." She took her gum out, looked at it, then stuck it back in her mouth. Angie wondered what she'd expected to see.

"I think she was here yesterday," End-is-near added. The others shrugged.

"I'm going to be helping her with a dinner for Algernon to launch his new book. Have you read it yet?"

"I didn't know he had a book. He's not a writer," X-Files exclaimed indignantly. "He's got brains. A scientist. Some people say he's a vision...vision...vision-something-or-other."

"Visionary?" Angie offered.

"He's the true one," End-is-near added. "Everybody else just fakes it. For the money. Like that Moss-head freak. What a rip-off artist."

"You mean MosSHAD?" Angie said, pronouncing it as she'd heard Derrick and the others.

"I mean Moss-head," he reiterated. "That's 'cause he's got moss instead of brains."

"Hey, did you guys hear about his botched-up abduction?" The gum-chewer stopped chomping long enough to ask the question. "People said he just walked out of the building. They saw him leave, but now the press is making a big deal out of it."

"Gross," End-is-near said. "Junk like that gives us all a bad name."

"He's such a phony, dude," X-files said. "So is that jerk he hangs around with? The pretty boy? You know the one."

"Derrick Holton," gum-chewer said. "He's sooo cute." She made a strange squealing sound. "Too bad he's on *their* side. He calls himself their president now."

"He's a phony, dude, if I ever saw one," X-files said.

"He's so phony he gives fakes a bad name," End-is-near pronounced.

As they chortled, gum-chewer swallowed her gum. "Oh, shit," she muttered, pounding her chest.

"Why do all of you think he's a fraud?" Connie's voice was filled with indignation. Angie's eyebrows rose—her friend was already defending Derrick, and they'd only spoken a few words. He had vanished after the "abduction" the other night, so they never did go out with him for drinks.

The Promethean three now eyed Connie as if she were some sort of spy. "We just know, dude," X-Files said. The other two nodded. "Algernon's no fraud, though. He's the real deal."

"He's cute, too. If you like older men," the ex-gum chewer said.

Angie wondered what the girl thought older consisted of. Anyone over thirty?

"So, are you gals interested in anything in particular?" End-is-near leaned forward, elbows on the counter. "Maybe we could help you out?"

Angie looked back at him. Well, she'd asked everyone else—why not them? "I do have a question. What do aliens eat?"

The three glanced at each other, then X-Files leaned close and said in a hushed voice, "Earthlings."

9

Another male. This victim seemed to be in his forties. This time, the entire genital area had been removed. It was done as cleanly and bloodlessly as the body found in Stern Grove. But here, the number five had been carved into the man's chest.

Paavo stood on the infield of the city's ballpark and looked down at the victim. He had come from the dugout where he'd talked to the security team and the groundkeepers who had found the body. They'd given him a good idea of what he would see when he got there. Maybe that was why, as he crossed the field, he'd taken the time for a detour to the pitcher's mound, stood on the rubber a quick second and stared at home plate. When he was a kid, his stepfather, Aulis Kokkonen, would take him to Giants' baseball games. He had dreamed of standing on the mound one day. He guessed this was as close as he'd ever get. Then he turned and hurried toward the crime scene.

As Yosh joined him, he looked once more down at the body. This one hadn't been dead a couple of days like Lambert. He was so recently killed his skin still smelled burnt where the cuts had been cauterized.

Paavo held his breath as he squatted down to better inspect the body. There was no lividity. Finger pressure could not turn the skin any whiter than it already was. It looked as if this victim, like the first, had been drained of blood. Rigor mortis was in the early development stage. Not many hours earlier, this man was still alive.

In the center of the victim's forehead, a small wafer-like metal object had been placed. Paavo didn't touch or move it until the photographers got there, just in case there was some significance to its position. It seemed to be some kind of computer circuitry, but neither Paavo nor Yosh, or any of the patrol officers around them, had any idea what they were looking at.

"It's got to be the same doer," Yosh said. "I don't want to think there's more than one psycho going around hacking up people like that."

"What worries me," Paavo said, "is that only about a week passed since the first killing, depending on how accurately we estimated the day of Lambert's murder." And only five days had passed since they had discovered the body and had put in numerous hours trying to find the killer. All they had to show for the time spent was another murder. Paavo shook his head in disgust.

He knew that anyone who killed so brutally usually took a few weeks, even months, between crimes. Past studies of serial and spree killers showed that such killings often accompanied a kind of sexual frenzy on the part of the killer. Those who mutilated their victims, in particular, went into a profound exhaustion for days thereafter. It was considered nearly impossible for someone to kill again in such a lurid way after only a matter of days. Nearly impossible, but obviously, not completely so.

Or—the thought was chilling—there might be more than

one killer. A cult, perhaps? One that had a sick fascination with death?

Equally grim was the possibility that these killings were being done without the frenzy and emotional involvement and release such horrid crimes usually afforded. Was it possible for a man to commit crimes like that without passion? To do it with indifference? Not, in Paavo's opinion, if the killer had any humanity at all.

Paavo slowly circled the victim. Needle marks speckled his arms. He was so skinny his ribs showed. From the filthy hair, to the battered and scarred hands with grimy, long nails, and the callused feet with ragged toenails, the corpse revealed the markings of a man who had lived hard and lived on the streets, the antithesis of the immaculate Bertram Lambert.

Just as with the last victim, something about the mutilation and the way the victim lay cast a ritualistic tinge over the murder.

"Number five," Yosh muttered, as much to himself as to his partner. "What the hell does it mean? The other guy had a seven. Seven, five? Seventy-five? I don't get it."

"It might be the start of an even bigger number," Paavo said.

"Let's hope it's not too big a number," Yosh said, his voice low. "I don't want to see any more vics end up like this."

Paavo silently scanned the empty ballpark. "Something tells me we're only looking at strike two."

10

Angie spent the day working on menus and suggested fantasy themes for her meeting with Triana and the mysterious Algernon. Their meeting had been set for 7 o'clock that evening at an apartment rented by the secretary of the Prometheus Group.

Angie also spent the day making sure her phone was charged and by her side in case Paavo called. Of course, he didn't, and she was growing more frustrated about him with every passing minute.

Finally, the time came for her meeting. Angie and Connie peered up at the large, dark and dreary apartment building on the part of Bush Street that lay between the gentrified area of Polk Street and the seedy porn shops and prostitute haunts of the Tenderloin. Angie double-checked the address Triana had texted her. This was where she was supposed to meet Algernon.

Angie had been nervous about going alone, and convinced Connie to go with her.

Now, Connie nervously hooked her arm in Angie's. "It looks kind of creepy from out here, but I'm sure it'll be fine inside. Can't judge a book by its cover. Ha, ha."

Angie glanced at her friend and grimaced. "We'll meet Algernon, talk about the event, and then leave," Angie said, mustering her courage.

"That's right. It'll help you plan his book launch." Connie straightened her back, lifting her chin as she pushed open the main door and entered the building. "And, if Derrick and I are to have a chance together, I need to understand him and everything he's involved in a lot better than I do now."

Angie had to agree with that. Derrick had phoned her that morning and said Dr. Mosshad still hadn't "reappeared," whatever that meant. He asked that she join him for lunch or perhaps for those cocktails he'd promised her and Connie. She turned him down, but suggested that Connie might be free, and gave him Connie's phone number. So far, he hadn't used it.

Now, with growing apprehension, Angie and Connie walked up the stairs to the Prometheus Group meeting in apartment six. The walls of the stairwell and hallways were painted black and the doors a garish red. No welcoming doorbell was evident. As Connie nodded encouragement, Angie knocked.

The door was opened by a woman wearing a soiled, sleeveless, floor-length Cleopatra-style outfit. Except that Cleopatra wouldn't have been caught dead in it. Tied around her head was a gold ribbon and sticking up from the center, over her forehead, was a small yellow plastic snake—the type that costs about ninety-nine cents at a dollar store.

It was all Angie could do to stop staring.

"Greetings, fellow voyagers," the woman bellowed. "I am Isis, daughter of the Great Pyramid. Welcome."

"I'm Angie, daughter of Sal and Serafina. This is Connie. We're here as guests of Triana Crisswell." The two moved cautiously into the apartment. The furniture was as rundown as the rest of the building. A blue Naugahyde sofa and chairs that must have been nearly fifty years old were in the center of the room. Didn't that stuff ever wear out? Wooden chairs filled the rest of the space. Three men and four women chatted and paid no attention to the new arrivals. Triana was not among them.

"Here it comes!" someone shouted. Everyone leaped from their chairs and circled a computer monitor.

"We're going to look at some pictures taken by members of our Santa Fe chapter while visiting Egypt," Isis explained. "Santa Fe is filled with good *feng shui* so sensitive people such as us can live there. Only a few places are suitable for us, you know."

"Is that so?" Connie asked, bobbing her head to see the computer screen.

"Yes. Santa Fe, Sedona, and of course, San Francisco and Berkeley."

There was nothing in the least bit spiritual or ethereal about Berkeley to Angie's eye. Or San Francisco, for that matter. She wondered if that was *feng shui* humor.

"It's beautiful!" one of the men shouted when the photo came clearly into view. Connie moved in close to get a better view. To Angie, though, it looked like all other photos she'd seen of the Great Pyramid. She once saw the real thing and photos didn't do it justice.

Angie watched the changing images for less than a minute, then stepped back to Isis, who remained near the door. Connie seemed to be as engrossed as the others watching the photos and listening to a running commentary about the chambers inside the pyramid.

"Why all this interest in the Great Pyramid?" Angie asked Isis. "Does this have to do with pyramid power, or whatever that is?"

"Not at all," a deep, male voice behind them said.

Angie turned to face the man who spoke. He was tall and darkly handsome with flowing black hair that reached his shoulders and a black suit that bore a close resemblance to the old Nehru jackets of fleeting popularity. "That was New Age nonsense," he said. "This is real. The Great Pyramid is so large it can be seen from the moon." His purple eyes fixed on Angie. Contacts, maybe? "Were you aware of that?"

"No, not really." She took a step back, as if pushed by the power of the man's eyes, contacts or not.

"The Great Pyramid's base is equal to seven midtown Manhattan blocks. Its weight is so great, only a solid stone mountain would be able to hold it—and the ancients built it right on top of solid granite. You must be a new member of our group," he said, taking her hand in both of his. His middle finger bore a heavy gold ring in the design of a cobra. "Tell me, Little Skeptic, how did such primitive people know that deep within the earth, far below the sand they chose, stood a mountain of solid granite?"

Mesmerized, Angie's gaze flitted between his purple eyes and the gold snake that coiled round and round his finger. "How did they?" she asked. This man had to be Algernon. There couldn't be two such powerful personalities in one group. She glanced toward the entrance. Where was Triana?

The man was already speaking. "It took a special knowledge, one impossible for them to possess"—his voice dropped dramatically—"on their own. It also took a special knowledge for the ancients to place the Great Pyramid in the exact center of the Earth's land mass."

Angie's brow furrowed. "The exact center?"

"Come." Holding her hand, he led her away from the others across the room to a desk with a globe of the world. She turned toward Connie, wanting to gesture for Connie to come with her, but Connie's attention was glued to the computer monitor.

With his right hand he slowly spun the globe. "East to west, the pyramid's axis corresponds to the longest land parallel across the earth." He stopped the globe with Egypt facing them.

"North to south, it passes through the longest land meridian on earth. In other words, out of three billion places where the Great Pyramid could have been built, the spot chosen was the one place where the greatest north-to-south and east-to-west land masses cross." He whispered in her ear. "How could the ancients have known that?"

She swallowed hard, both intrigued by what this man was saying, but also alarmed by him. He exuded a strange energy. Some might have found it sexual, but to her, it was too much, as if he was trying so hard to be alluring, she found herself repulsed. "I don't know," she finally responded.

He wore a closed-mouthed, indulgent smile as he lightly touched her shoulders and turned her to face him. Gazing down at her, he slid his hands to her arms as he spoke. "The total length of the Great Pyramid's base is a precise fraction of the earth's circumference, and the ratio of the height to its base perimeter is the same as the earth's radius to its circumference. How could ancient Egyptians have known that?"

She couldn't even follow what he said, let alone be able to answer. Her thoughts were on his too-warm hands holding her. *Where the hell is Triana?* She was about to quit this job and leave.

"When you look at the stars, Little Skeptic," he said, moving closer and capturing her gaze, "the positioning of the pyramids is mathematically proportional to how the constellation of Orion would have appeared in the sky in 10500 B. C."

"That's very long ago," she murmured, on the verge of bolting.

"Old doesn't begin to do it justice." The harsh female voice coming from behind Angie broke the growing tension Angie felt. The strange man dropped his hands and moved back as Isis stepped between them. Her eyes burned. "The pyramids were built at that time, you know."

Angie felt as if she could breathe again. Also, the building of the pyramids was something she *did* know, having studied about Egypt before visiting it while she was living in Rome. "The pyramids were built twenty-five hundred years before Christ, not ten thousand."

"That's old thinking," Isis sneered. "New, places them much older. Archaeologists discovered that a vent in the King's Chamber points to Orion, the sacred home of Osiris, the Egyptian god. A vent in the Queen's Chamber points to Sirius —the star sacred to Osiris's consort Isis."

"Isn't Osiris the god of the dead?" Angie asked, trying to remember the Egyptian theology she'd once learned a little about. Her gaze went again to the dark stranger as she pointedly turned her back on Isis.

"Life and death spring from each other," he said, meeting Angie's eyes. "One could say the pyramids, too, are as connected with death as with immortality. In that sense it is a death cult."

Angie's eyebrows rose at the disquieting statement. Isis put her hand on Angie's arm. "We are its priest and priestess. Osiris and Isis, the lovers." She gazed fondly at the man, then back to Angie. "Let me introduce Osiris."

Angie glanced up at him. "Oh? I thought you were Algernon."

"I am." He gave her a small bow, and that same, haunting smile. "In a past life I was Osiris, Little Skeptic," he said. "But in this life, I am called Algernon."

"I'm here to meet you and Triana Crisswell, but it seems she hasn't made it here yet. I'm Angie Amalfi." She put out her hand to shake his. Looking bemused, he said nothing, but took her hand and shook it, using a surprisingly weak grasp. "I'm putting on the Fantasy Dinner… or buffet, I guess it is now… for your book signing… or not signing. Anyway, happy to meet you."

He chuckled and now grasped both her hands. "Well, no

wonder you are so skeptical, then. I was wondering how someone such as you had found her way to us."

Connie chose that moment to look up. Angie freed her hands and waved Connie over. Connie's eyes widened when she noticed Algernon.

As the two met, Angie took the opportunity to better study the man now that she knew for sure who he was. He was a lot older than she had first assumed. His skin had the too tight look usually associated with women who'd had facelifts, and his hair was too black to be natural. His neck and hands most gave his age away. Still, natural or not, he was a handsome man and, she could see that for some women, he probably did have the sex appeal Triana Crisswell had spoken of.

"It's so nice to meet you," Connie said. "I've been to NAUTS lectures and have heard so much about you."

A hard look passed over his eyes and then was gone. It was chilling and Angie hoped she had only imagined it. "You went to the NAUTS and learned about me?" Black eyes darted between Angie and Connie, but then he burst out laughing. "Did they have anything good to say?"

"Are you rivals, or what?" Angie asked, careful not to answer his question.

"Rivals denotes equals," he replied. "I'm afraid jealousy has more to do with our differences than anything. When the first leader of the Prometheans died, I took over. That was how he would have wanted it. Frederick Mosshad hated that I beat him out as the successor to I.M. Neumann, our founder, and left us to start the NAUTS. But Mosshad was weak, not a leader. Derrick Holton recently took over as president, but he'll only speed up the group's demise. The NAUTS are small and their philosophy is wrong. They have no followers to speak of, and so resort to stunts like that ridiculous alien abduction of Mosshad to get attention. It makes us all look like con men."

"What if Mosshad's disappearance wasn't a sham?" Connie

asked, clearly not liking him impugning Derrick Holton. "Mosshad hasn't returned yet."

Algernon shrugged. "More drama? Who cares? The Prometheans and I know the truth about the universe and the future. There is more to the universe than most men can imagine. The Ancients, the Egyptians, understood it, and so do I. I am followed by many. I am the truth."

Angie all but gasped aloud at the man's audacity.

"And Derrick Holton?" Connie asked, her lips firm.

"A gnat. To be swatted."

A gnat? Angie could scarcely believe what she was hearing. Connie looked ready to unleash a defense of Derrick, so she grabbed Connie's arm, excused them both, and hurried her out the door.

Derrick Holton lay in his bed, fast asleep, even as his eyes suddenly opened.

The bedroom was dark, but a light flickered and he heard a high, whining noise. He covered his ears with his hands and at the same time struggled into a sitting position. It didn't help, though, because the sound wasn't coming from the outside. It came from within him. Not again, he thought.

He knew with absolute certainty what was causing the lights, the sounds in his head. And he was afraid.

A white light shone into his window, dim at first, quickly growing brighter.

His mind screamed in fright. They were back, out there, taking people, wanting to take him.

He thought he'd managed to hide from them. He was wrong. He had to run. As he got off the bed he fell, tangled in his bedcovers. The clothes he'd worn yesterday were lying in a heap on a chair. He crawled to them, ignoring the painful sound in his ears.

He wouldn't let them take him. He'd die before he let them touch him again.

Clutching his clothes and shoes in his arms, he ran out to the apartment building's hallway, pulling his door shut behind him. Not that it mattered much. A closed door meant nothing to *them*.

He took the stairs down three flights to the basement parking garage. To his car.

He had to go somewhere they couldn't find him. Somewhere until he came up with a way to stop them. Somewhere to be safe. Somewhere far away now that, once again, *they were here.*

He got into his car and then slept free of dreams.

11

Paavo and Yosh were furious, but not nearly as much as Homicide's Lieutenant Hollins, the chief of police, or the mayor. Someone had leaked a report to the *San Francisco Chronicle*. The paper immediately blasted out a story that a mutilated body had been found at the Giants' ballpark. Newsmen from all over the Bay Area descended on the Hall of Justice as well as City Hall for more information. That morning, the print edition of the *Chronicle* reported, above the fold, everything the reporters had found out, causing a flurry of paranoia in an already nervous city.

And then, calls about missing persons began.

The number of people who had gone missing whose disappearance had never been reported to the Missing Persons Bureau always amazed homicide inspectors. Apparently, people didn't want to "get involved," or to answer all the questions a missing person's investigation could entail. But they were willing to call and ask if an unidentified murder victim fit the description of their missing loved one—or not-so-loved one.

Fortunately, for Paavo and Yosh, this victim had fingerprints on file so the identification was quickly made. He'd been picked up a few times for stealing booze and cigarettes. His rap sheet provided a name, Felix Rolfe, and that he'd been given a dishonorable discharge from the Army.

With some digging, they'd found that Rolfe was a drifter who lived on Supplemental Security Income for disability. He'd drifted throughout Nevada and Arizona for years, and finally came to California where the weather was milder and the SSI state supplement more generous. Most of his SSI money went to drugs and alcohol, which contributed to the liver disease that gave him the SSI disability, which allowed him to continue with his drug and alcohol habit.

The only address on record was his mother's—a rooming house on Third Street. As Paavo knocked on the door to her room, he braced himself for the need to deal with a distraught mother. He should have saved himself the trouble.

He sat on a wooden chair with plaid foam rubber cushions on the seat and back. Maureen Rolfe sat on the bed. She was an enormous woman with gray hair raggedly cut below her ears. Huge thighs forced her knees wide apart and caused the skirt of her worn blue dress to ride up too high. Black socks and men's shoes adorned her feet, and she smoked the butt of a stogie.

"Felix's killer put the number five on his chest. Does that number mean anything to you?" Paavo asked after a short talk during which he gave his condolences for Rolfe's untimely death. She had shrugged them off.

Now, she sucked on the cigar. "Number five? Why'd anyone want to carve up Fe?"

"That's what we're trying to find out. Did five have any significance you can think of?"

"Nope."

"Where did he live?" The fact that Bertram Lambert lived

on Seventh Avenue and the number seven had been carved on his chest, hadn't been lost on Paavo.

"On the streets."

When he asked where she would have looked for him had she needed to find him, she spit into an old coffee can and asked what it was worth to him.

Ten dollars got him the answer. The Giants' ballpark. Felix Rolfe had found it a good place to panhandle.

When Angie awoke the next morning, she was nearly as tired as when she went to sleep. Things just weren't working out the way she had hoped they would. The man who should be the star attraction for her first Fantasy Dinner troubled her greatly. He was fascinating, seemed intelligent, and she was sure some would call him charismatic. But he came on too strong with her.

And the worship of death, even if it was in the classic Egyptian form of Osiris, was disturbing to her on many levels, both social and spiritual, having been raised a Catholic in her family's very old-world Italian way. When Algernon said, "I am the truth," it reminded her of the Gospel of John, "I am the way, the truth, and the life." Algernon's words had chilled her.

The bad blood between him and Derrick also concerned her. Derrick had changed a lot since she'd known him, but basically, he seemed to still be the good person she had once dated, just a bit mixed up now with this UFO nonsense. Still, she gave store to his feelings about Algernon.

She needed to rethink her involvement in Algernon's party. The people around him were too strange for her taste. She decided to phone Triana and bow out.

Just then her phone rang. Triana Crisswell's name showed up on the screen. Good timing.

"Hello," she said.

"Angie? This is Triana Crisswell."

"Yes, I was just thinking about you. I—"

"So sorry about last night! I would have been there except my husband came home early and started up again about my friends. He just doesn't understand the Prometheus Group. He gave me such a headache, I had to take to my bed! Anyway, I talked to Algernon this morning. And you made such a hit with him, I can't tell you! I've rarely heard him so excited about anyone. Not only was he impressed with you, but with me for finding you. You're a pro, Miss Amalfi. I'm going to tell all my friends about you."

"Oh?" How was she going to bow out now? She took a deep breath. "That's very nice, but—"

"No need to thank me. We're up to three hundred people already! And I haven't done any publicity to speak of. This party is going to be bigger and more important than ever."

"I'm really sorry, but—"

"Don't be! It's that much more exciting this way! It means your hard work will be seen and valued by even more people. Your name will be made with this event, sweetie. You better believe it."

That's exactly what she was afraid of. She guessed she was stuck putting on the dinner, after all.

"One more little thing," Triana continued. "Algernon wants to get together to discuss this party with you personally."

"He does?"

"This is such an honor! He's even willing to come to your house. He, uh, suggested that since I'm so busy, I don't need to be there, so don't worry about me. What would be a good time for the two of you to meet?"

So that's his game. "Why, Mrs. Crisswell, I couldn't possibly meet with him unless you were there as well," Angie said. "In fact, I wouldn't dream of it."

"Oh, isn't that sweet of you, Angie! I'd love to join you both—if you're sure. Algernon sounded as if he thought I might not be needed, and I certainly wouldn't want to be in the way."

"Don't be silly, you couldn't possibly be anything but a welcome addition. My time is your time. Give me a call when you settle on a time that you're both available."

"I'll be in touch, Angie. And, how is the planning coming?"

"Wonderfully, just wonderfully. Let's talk about it when you're here."

"I'm so pleased. Call me if you need me. Tah-tah!"

With that, she hung up.

Angie just sat for a few minutes staring at the phone. How had she gotten into this fix? All she wanted to do was to have a simple little business. Cater some fun dinners for people. Throw a few parties. That's all. Instead she was going to end up feeding all the nut cases in the Bay Area.

And one creepy Egyptian god.

Triana was right about one thing, though. The people attending this party would be the crème de la crème of San Francisco. They might be wacko crème, but crème nonetheless. And crème always gave big dinner parties, needing to hire people just like her to help out.

Somehow, she might make a go of this business, yet.

A shave-and-a-haircut knock on the door to her apartment came as a welcome distraction.

"Stan! What in the world?" She stared at her neighbor from across the hall, then backed up as he entered her apartment.

"Angie, I'm desperate. Do you have anything to eat? I can't go to a restaurant looking like this. In fact, not even to the corner grocery. I haven't eaten all day today." In each ear, Stan had stuck a piece of aluminum foil, twisted the size and shape of a cigarette.

"Tell me, Stanfield," Angie said calmly, "why do you have tin foil stuck in your ears?"

"I can explain... after I've eaten." He gave her a doe-eyed, hollow-cheeked look, like a starving waif in a Keane painting. Angie knew he was anything but starving, considering that he mooched meals throughout the apartment building, and probably from people at work as well.

"Check the fridge." Angie said. "My mother —"

"What? You'll have to speak up a bit," Stan said, his back to her as he dashed toward the kitchen. "The foil, you know."

"My mother sent my sister Bianca over with a care package for me, some left-over cannelloni from a big dinner party. If you aren't interested in that, there's some yogurt. Or, you can open a can of tuna, throw in some curry powder and sour cream, and—"

"No, no!" Stan shuddered at the thought and pulled open the door of the refrigerator. "I have nothing against leftovers." As he stuck his head inside to check out the goodies, one of the pieces of foil hit the side and fell to the floor. He straightened up and reattached it. Then, squatting slightly, he continued his search for the cannelloni—pasta tubes filled with ricotta and Parmesan cheese, chunks of chicken, ground veal, and spices, then covered with a red sauce and teleme cheese—along with any other food that might find its way to his stomach. "I wonder if I dare use your microwave with this tin foil?"

"I think you'll be fine as long as you don't stick your head in it," Angie replied dryly. "Why are you wearing those things, anyway?"

"Headaches. I couldn't even go to work the other day because of them." Clearly deciding to brave the dangers of the microwave, he put the pasta in and set it on high for two minutes.

"So you're trying to prove your case for disability benefits, is that it? If you don't get them for physical, you will for mental." With the microwave oven humming and the aluminum foil in his ears he didn't seem to hear her.

He got himself a fork, a napkin and a glass of red wine. He liked wine with Italian food.

She mixed a green salad with a simple olive oil, onion, garlic, oregano and Balsamic vinegar dressing for him and brought it and the wine out to the dining room table, closely followed by Stan, gingerly carrying the hot plate of food.

He sat down and took a big bite. "Delicious. You're a good cook, Angie, but your mother is really outstanding."

"Uh huh." She'd heard that before. More times than she could count. It didn't do her attitude about Stan any good to hear him praise the food she'd been saving for her own dinner later that night.

Maybe this was God's way of telling her to start the diet she'd been thinking about.

Although she had more important things to do than to pay attention to Stan, her curiosity got the better of her. "Why do you think tin foil will stop a headache?" she asked, even while knowing the answer would probably make little sense.

"At my gym yesterday, I met a girl, a woman I should say, who went to a big sci-fi conference at the Moscone Center. She was talking to me all about UFOs and aliens. Did you know they send a lot of mysterious waves into our atmosphere? Metal helps block them."

As predicted. "Now, wait a minute. You think aliens are sending out some kind of waves that give you headaches?"

"It's true! I had it confirmed listening to podcast she recommended. This guy, Algernon, was being interviewed. He talked about all the strange stuff that goes on in the world that we have no explanation for. The explanation, he said, is that it's all being controlled by aliens. And they're working with the government. Or they've taken over the government, not sure which. Anyway, one of the ways they control us is with those waves. The more sensitive among us—like me—feel them, and get headaches."

"You said his name was Algernon? What did you think of him?"

"He was great! He's got a new book coming out. I'm hoping the library gets a copy."

"What about the woman who told you about all this? Does she like Algernon?"

"I don't know."

"Could you ask her?"

"I don't think I'll see her again. Frankly, she creeped me out with all her talk about extraterrestrial stuff. Do you know some lecturer was abducted right here in the city? And now, even though the police are hiding it, aliens not only abducted but murdered two men and mutilated their bodies! It's all too scary. That's another reason I don't want to go out. It's way too dangerous out there. You might want to use some tinfoil, too."

A satisfied look suddenly filled his face as he polished off the entire plate of cannelloni, making "mmm" sounds. She was ready to smack him, but then his words registered.

"What do you mean about murdered men and mutilated bodies?"

"It's in the paper this morning. Didn't your boyfriend tell you about it? Oh, wait, you aren't seeing him anymore, are you?"

She gritted her teeth as she grabbed her computer tablet and opened it to the *Chronicle*. "Oh, my God," she muttered as she read the article. If Paavo was involved in a case this ugly, that could be a reason for his absences and strange behavior. At least, maybe…

"I don't see the connection with aliens, Stan," she said, scanning the article again.

"It has to do with cattle mutilations. The woman I mentioned told me about them, and crop circles. The aliens come down to Earth, make circles in farmers' fields, and carve out the insides of cows and bulls. Heaven only knows why.

Apparently, those men were mutilated the same way. Got to be aliens. And, to think, I used to do find ET so cute when I was a kid." He wiped his mouth on his napkin and then stood. "Thanks for the meal. I feel better now. See you later."

Taking a couple of macaroons, he left the apartment.

Much as Angie hated to admit it, Stan might have been right. EBEs, aliens, whatever, they were all weird, as were Algernon, Derrick, and the rest of their friends. Could any of them be dangerous too? No, she couldn't imagine that, but still this was a wake-up call for her.

She was especially worried about Connie. Her friend was a little too besotted by Derrick's good looks, in her opinion.

She and Connie needed to have a heart-to-heart.

Angie picked up the phone and called Everyone's Fancy. Connie's part-time clerk, Lyssa, answered. "Connie's gone," she replied to Angie's question.

"Gone? Where has she gone?"

"To buy a new dress. She's going to a talk tonight at a place called Tardis Hall. I've never heard of it, but she's apparently meeting some guy there, and she wants to look good."

Angie was sure of the answer, but she had to ask, "Did she say what kind of meeting?"

"I'm not sure. I think she said something about UFOs. I didn't listen. It sounded, like, far out there, you know?"

Angie hung up. What had she gotten Connie into?

12

"Beware, the end is near!" The stout, Hitler-mustached man shouted the words to people passing Tardis Hall. He waved his UFO brochures. "Join our group as we seek the safety of a new world. Learn what the government isn't telling you: the end is near!"

A gray-haired African-American man strode by looking at the Hall as he went.

"This is for you, brother," the speaker cried, holding out a brochure.

The man gave him of look of disdain. "I'm no brother of yours unless a miracle happened."

The speaker forced a chuckle. "You pay attention to things of no importance, like the color of skin, when soon, our differences will be nothing in the face of the enemy of all humankind. We will be side by side, and we will be brothers. Believe me. It's all here, in this flyer." He waggled the brochure about Roswell. "And, you just might win a hundred dollars, besides." He pointed to the sign.

New members! Free drawings!

$100 to the lucky winner! Join today!

The man studied the brochure a moment. "Does your group also talk about other things? Area 51, for instance?"

"Absolutely. Are you familiar with Area 51?"

The man hesitated, then replied, "A bit."

"Join us, then. It only costs five dollars, which is deducted from the price of tonight's lecture, so it's basically free. And even if you never come to a meeting, this is a chance to win a hundred dollars."

"So, it costs nothing to join, and if I win, I get a hundred bucks?"

"That's right."

The man's brow furrowed as he studied the brochure. "Why not?" He picked up the BIC pen on the table and filled out a card for the drawing.

The speaker glanced at the address, phone number, and at the name—Leon Cole.

"I think you have a wonderful chance at winning, Mr. Cole," he said. "This phone number is good to reach you at, right?"

"You call and tell me I've won, and I'll make any damn phone number you want be the right one."

That evening, Angie hurried into Tardis Hall. She needed to find Connie and suggest her friend forget about any interest in Derrick Holton until they were sure he and his bizarre NAUTS group was on the up and up.

The first thing she noticed was a table with food and beverages spread out on it. Paper cups, a punch bowl with lemonade, and platters of thin pretzel sticks and goldfish-shaped crackers were offered. Angie couldn't imagine serving anything so uncreative. If this was the kind of catering a UFO group was used to, she wouldn't have to work hard at all to win praise for the party she was planning for Triana.

"Hello."

Angie turned at the voice and saw the chubby fellow with the ugly little Hitler mustache who was usually outdoors hawking Roswell brochures and a hundred-dollar drawing. He flicked the bottom of his daisy-patterned tie as he spoke. "You're new here, but I've seen you before. You should think about joining us. You might even win a hundred dollars." His smile made his chubby cheeks dimple deeply. "My name is John Oliver Harding. But everyone here calls me Oliver Hardy." He gripped his shirt as if it were a vest and waggled his fingers. "I'm into old movies and comedies."

"Ah, I see," Angie said, stepping back a bit. She got it. Laurel and Hardy. Very old, indeed. "But aren't you usually outside trying to get people to join your sweepstakes?"

"It started to rain again. Here's a brochure." He handed her one about Roswell.

She dropped it in her handbag. "I'm looking for Derrick Holton. Have you seen him?" She scanned the small group once more for Connie or Derrick.

"I guess you and Derrick are an item?" Oliver asked, stepping closer.

"We're not." Her tone was curt. "I knew him a few years ago."

"That doesn't mean you can't go out with him now!" He sounded almost angry.

She was taken aback by his vehemence. "I'm seeing someone else." She clamped her mouth shut as if to say, end of story.

Instead, he twisted his head from side to side. "Not that I'd notice. If you were my girlfriend, I'd be with you."

Fat chance. "I'm afraid he's busy. He's a homicide inspector," she said pointedly. "He's investigating those mutilation murders."

Oliver's eyes widened. "Mutilation murders?"

Sheesh, as if the whole city wasn't talking about them. "The ones on the front page of today's paper. And they keep posting updates as more information breaks."

"I don't read the news." Oliver shook his head, causing his cheeks to jiggle. "It's too depressing. Especially if someone's murdering women. I keep away from them. I'm too sensitive for this world, I'm afraid."

She seemed to be hearing a lot about sensitive males these days. "They aren't young women, they're men."

"Men?" His face turned milky white. "Are you sure?"

"That's what the papers say. They aren't reporting the first victim's name, but he was found at Sigmund Stern Grove. In the second was found at Giants' Stadium, of all places."

She stopped speaking. Oliver had gone from pale to green and now looked as if he were going to pass out. "Are you all right?"

"Y-yes. Do you know the second man's name?"

"The paper said Felix Rolfe."

"Felix..." He whispered.

"Did you know him?" she asked.

"Me? No. Never heard of him. Not at all. But... but why is homicide involved? Do people think they were murdered?"

"Of course, they were. All the evidence shows they were murdered by some very sick human."

"Are you sure?"

This guy was even more wigged out than most of the UFO types. "I suggest you get today's paper, or look online, and read it yourself."

"Oh, my." He pressed his hands to his stomach. "Excuse me, please. I told you things like that upset me. That's why I don't read or listen to the news anymore."

He turned and rushed away from her.

Shaking her head, she went inside the auditorium to find a seat and hopefully, Derrick and Connie.

But no sooner had she sat down in the back row of the auditorium than a familiar face appeared, and once again, sat down beside her.

"Hello, Malachi," she said to the gaunt, bearded, gray-haired man she'd met at her first visit to Tardis Hall. He was again dressed in a black turtleneck and black slacks. "Are you here to see another abduction?"

"Absolutely." He gave her a wink. "I haven't had so much fun in years."

She laughed. She had no idea if he took the abduction seriously or not, but he was having a good time with it no matter what.

"But why are you here again?" he asked. "Surely, you have better things to do than to spend time with people who have so much trouble dealing with this world they search for a better one in the stars."

She was surprised to hear him say that. "Aren't you being unfair? These might simply be people with an overblown imagination."

He grinned. "I stand corrected... somewhat."

She smiled as well. He seemed to be the most logical person in this entire hall. "Last time we talked you told me about the rift between Derrick and Algernon. I met Algernon. What a piece of work."

Malachi chuckled. "Algernon is all show. He wouldn't know a flying saucer from a turnip. And frankly, I believe he's more interested in women than in any EBE, which isn't to say an alien female would be safe around him. Why do you care at all about Algernon? You surely don't want to join the Prometheans, do you?"

"I've been asked to host a theme party for Algernon's book

launch. Since I have a new business, I wanted to do it right. The right theme, the right food. But, with this Algernon, I just don't know..."

He seemed to think a moment, then cocked his head. "I'll tell you, you won't go wrong with these people if you use the crash at Roswell as your theme. Everyone is fascinated by it... and by what happened after the crash."

"Really?" she said as she watched Derrick step up to the microphone. But where was Connie?

Malachi leaned closer. "Just think of the sudden blossoming of technology in our society—the rudimentary things we had before World War Two, and how, a very few years after, we're in a computer and technological age unimaginable just seventy years ago." As Derrick began to speak, Malachi dropped his voice to a whisper. "Transistors, lasers, even Saran Wrap, all exist because of Roswell."

Angie wanted to ask more about Saran Wrap, but the speaker was introduced to some applause, and he immediately began his lecture. Derrick stepped backstage instead of joining the audience. Angie wondered if Connie was back there, too.

The speaker, whose name Angie didn't catch, had a high, thin voice that rose and fell as he spoke, making his words hard to understand. He showed slides of Mars and spoke of how a replica of a human face had been built on it by ancient aliens who used the face to remind those who ventured to Earth of their true home.

She wondered how the speaker knew that, as he showed more and more slides, droning on and on about the beings who built the face, and how intelligent they were, and where they were now.

Suddenly, someone was shaking her arm. She hadn't realized she'd fallen asleep, but she opened her eyes to find Derrick beside her. "It's over," he said with a grin.

She saw that people were putting on coats and leaving the

hall. She rubbed her eyes. She must have been really tired so sleep so soundly. But then, maybe everyone had been lulled into quietly leaving. Like Malachi must have done. Derrick now sat in his chair.

She gathered her things. "I'm sorry. I didn't mean to fall asleep this way. How embarrassing!"

He grinned. "Nothing you do could be an embarrassment, Angelina. In fact, I'm flattered you came to see me." He ran his fingers through his hair, rumpling it as he twisted this way and that looking over the rapidly emptying lecture hall. "Tell you what, why don't we go out for coffee after I close up the auditorium? Looks like you could use a cup. Then we can talk."

"That would be great." She glanced around. "Where's Connie?"

"Connie? I don't know. I haven't seen her. Let's go backstage." He took her arm. "It'll only take me about ten minutes to shut down the place, then we'll get out of here."

Angie walked with him onto the stage, and Derrick opened the red drapery backdrop to reveal an enormous backstage area. She'd forgotten that Tardis Hall had originally been built as a warehouse. Only a small portion of it—the entrance area, the auditorium, and the stage area—had been finished off and painted.

The entire backstage looked like the warehouse it was, with lots of heavy standalone shelves, some filled with boxes, and most empty. Metal staircases led to upper floors, and a side elevator had the wide-door look of those that carry freight.

In all, backstage was a cavernous, dark, unfriendly place. She understood why the drapery was used to block it from being seen.

Derrick led her to a chair to wait for him, then darted off. She pulled out her cell phone and punched in Connie's number.

"Hello," Connie answered.

"Where are you?" Angie shrieked. "Lyssa told me you'd be at Tardis Hall so I'm here waiting for you! I just listened to a lecture about a face on Mars!"

"Why are you doing that?" Connie asked. "I went to buy a new outfit first, but everything made me look fat. So I decided to starve for a couple of days before seeing Derrick again. No more tiramisu for me. So, what's up?"

Angie realized that now was not the time to discuss her concerns about Derrick. Besides, she might be overreacting. Sometimes she did that.

"Nothing special," she said as she saw Derrick approach. "Time for me to head home. I'll talk to you tomorrow." She hung up.

"We'll leave as soon as I can lock up the hall," Derrick said, as he paced back and forth like a caged tiger. Soon Elvis, the well-dressed young man Angie had met earlier, and Sir Galahad of the weird speech pattern, joined them.

"All set to get out of here?" Elvis asked.

"Sir Oliver is not here as yet," Galahad said, holding a broom upright as if it were a shepherd's staff. "He is probably asleepeth somewhere. I should think the face on Mars controversy sent him to slumberland. It has not aged well. Forsooth, I nearly fell asleep on the projector."

"I did fall asleep," Angie confessed. "Maybe Oliver went home?"

"Not without telling us," Derrick said. "He's got to be sleeping somewhere here. Let's call and wake him up."

They all walked around yelling his name. Angie found it spooky the way "Oliver" reverberated through the former warehouse.

"I'm getting nervous," she said to Derrick. "Do your friends often go missing this way?" She couldn't imagine anyone with Oliver's girth and odd looks not having his every move noticed by someone.

"They never have before." Derrick rubbed his hair, making it even more askew. "I'm going to look around some more. He might be hurt. I don't know why he didn't hear when we called him."

"I hope he wasn't abducted, too," Elvis said. He went in a different direction from Derrick.

"I'd better help, too," Galahad mumbled, forgetting his "accent," as he walked away.

Oliver couldn't seriously have disappeared, Angie thought. Although he was quite upset by the mutilation murders, so maybe he did go home. She wished she had mentioned that to the others.

She poked around here and there herself, but then stopped, realizing that everyone had walked off to search, and left her here alone. She wished she had simply said goodbye to Derrick and left. Next time she saw him, she would do just that.

Considering how big the warehouse was, if Oliver wandered off very far and either fell asleep or got hurt, it could take a long time to find him. She went to the open stairway. The stairs seemed to go up one or two floors. The only lights were a few emergency lights around the stairs itself, to prevent accidents. She shuddered. The building gave her a bad feeling when people were in it. Empty, it was like something out of a teenage horror movie—*Nightmare in Tardis Hall.*

The big building was empty and, according to Triana, would be destroyed soon to make way for redevelopment. The thought of wandering around in it looking for someone was not her idea of fun.

She hurried away from the stairs. Not sure what else to do, she opened a nearby door, turned on the lights, and looked inside.

It was an empty storeroom. She stepped out again and shut the door. She would ask Derrick if anyone had checked to see if Oliver's car was gone. If Oliver had a car, that is. Now, she couldn't even hear anyone's footsteps. No wonder, in a building this large.

She returned to the backstage area where they'd met earlier.

It was certainly quiet in here. She wished someone would come back. They wouldn't have all gone home and left her here, would they? They weren't pranksters, she hoped. On the other hand, where were they?

The backstage lights were still on. That told her they must still be searching for Oliver, didn't it? Nothing to get alarmed about.

But then she heard footsteps back in warehouse area. Running footsteps. "Hello!" she called. "Have you found him?"

No answer. Why not? And why was someone running around here? Where was everyone? "Hello? Derrick? Oliver? Is anyone there?"

Still no answer. Why weren't they answering unless... like Mosshad... they had all been....

No! No one has been abducted by aliens!

She was appalled such a thought had even crossed her mind. The bizarre beliefs of these people were more infectious than she had imagined.

Should she search for them? No way. She'd watched enough scary movies to know better than to go walking into dark, dank areas all by herself. She'd wait here. That was the safest thing to do.

Not far from where she stood, she saw restroom doors marked Men and Women. She decided to quickly use the facilities while waiting for Derrick.

The women's room was dark, but a light switch was right next to the entry. She flipped it up.

The light came on, showing an old bathroom with two stalls and a single sink with a mirror over it. The stall doors were slightly ajar, as if someone had pulled them shut, but not all the way.

A pool of red liquid lay in a puddle in the center of the bathroom floor. As she stepped closer and stared at the liquid, a mounting horror stole over her. A drop fell into the pool.

A drop of blood. Coming from...

Afraid, yet at the same time unable to stop herself, she raised her eyes to the ceiling.

A glass skylight was overhead. Splayed against it lay Oliver Hardy, his face pressed hard against the cracked glass as blood oozed from his mouth and nose, his eyes open and unfocussed with the look of death.

She ran out of the bathroom and then, needing Derrick and anyone else nearby to hear her, screamed loud enough to wake the dead.

13

Paavo and Yosh were finishing up another long day in Homicide. With two ugly deaths, plus the press being involved, their work had more than doubled, but they were still dealing with crime scenes that had been staged, and so far, had offered no help.

Even the security cameras at the Giants ballpark had caught nothing of note.

Just then Paavo's phone rang. He scarcely said hello when Angie's words tumbled out, loud and excited. "Paavo, come quick. There's a dead body. And I found him! I thought they'd send you to investigate, but instead they sent some bossy blonde and some spooky guy who stands on the sidelines and twitches. Please, we need you here."

He jumped to his feet, gripping the phone tighter. Angie with a dead body? Her words made little sense—except for her description of Homicide Inspectors Rebecca Mayfield and Bill Never-Take-A-Chance Sutter, tonight's on-call homicide team. "Where are you?"

"Tardis Hall at the foot of Brannan."

"You're there *again?*"

"I... Connie... well, I came to another lecture." Her voice was small. "Afterward, Oliver Hardy disappeared. That's not his real name, but I can't remember what his real name is. Everyone else went to look for him, except me. I went to the women's room. And there he was! I mean, he wasn't *in* the women's room. But that's not important. You need to come and find out what's going on here!"

"Slow down. You found a body." He glanced up to see that Yosh was now also standing, a concerned expression on his face. "Did it look like an accident? Or, I should say, was there anything that made you think it might not have been a natural death?"

"I wouldn't call it natural. He was *outside* the building, on a skylight. And his head hit it with enough force to crack it and to kill him, I suspect."

"Damn! Angie, listen to me. You don't know those people well, so keep away from everyone but Inspector Mayfield. Understand? Inspector Rebecca Mayfield. She knows what she's doing."

"Seems to me she's doing a terrible job."

"Angie!" He stopped himself, sucking in his breath as he ran his free hand through his hair. "Just"—he was a little calmer now—"just do what I say. Stick to Mayfield. I'll be there as fast as I can."

He hung up the phone and grabbed his jacket, struggling to shove his arm through the sleeve while he talked to Yosh. "Angie's with some UFO nuts in a converted warehouse down on Brannon. One of them was found flattened on the roof, on a skylight. I've got to make sure she's all right."

"She does know how to get in the thick of things, doesn't she? UFO nuts, huh?" Yosh said trying not to chuckle as he put down his report and twisted the cap onto his pen.

"No need for you to come along." Paavo flipped his jacket collar down, checked his gun, and patted his pockets for his ID, keys, and phone. "Mayfield and Sutter are already at the scene. These mutilation murders need all your attention. Checking on Angie will be the extent of my involvement."

"I'll believe that when I see it," Yosh said, easing back in his chair. Then he chuckled. "Landed on a skylight, you said? Sounds like the guy might have been tossed out of a spaceship. Or, should I say, a flying saucer?"

Paavo stopped his Mustang in front of the entrance to Tardis Hall and ran inside. There wasn't anything for him to feel so frantic about. No reason to think Angie could be in danger—in one of the highest crime areas of the city—possibly with a murderer in the building with her or lurking nearby.

He shoved the doors open, flashed his badge at the patrol officer guarding the crime scene and sighed with relief when he saw Angie running toward him, arms waving. Behind her, open doors led to a large auditorium. All the lights were on.

"Paavo, thank God you're here!" she cried as she ran into his arms. "You can't imagine how horrible this has been! There was so much blood. And his eyes!"

He held her close a moment, breathing in the familiar scent of roses that was always around her, filling him with memories. But then he forced himself to step back to better check on her. "Are you all right?" he asked. She nodded, but wore a pinched, fearful look. He couldn't help but put his arms around her once more, holding her close until her trembling stopped.

Rebecca Mayfield, the city's only female homicide inspector, walked up to them. She was tall and graceful, with straight blonde hair, pulled back in a pony tail. "What took you so long?" she asked Paavo. She stood with one hand on her hip.

"You knew I was coming?"

Rebecca gave Angie a glance, then cocked an eyebrow. "I

had no doubt about it, Inspector, since you know one of our prime suspects."

All the blood drained from Angie's face. She spun toward Rebecca. "Your what?" Her words were strangled.

"She's joking, Angie," Paavo said, shooting Rebecca an icy glare.

Rebecca folded her arms. "The person who finds the body is always a prime suspect," she said matter-of-factly. "That's one of the first lessons in homicide investigation. You know that, Inspector Smith."

Before he had a chance to respond, Angie blurted out, "That is the most blatantly foolish—"

He took her arm and drew her away, not in the least amused by Rebecca's antics. "Let's go."

Rebecca couldn't help but smile and shake her head before she hurried off to continue with her investigation.

Paavo went with Angie into the auditorium. The stage lights were lit, drapery open to reveal the large warehouse. Several patrol officers stood guard and crime scene tape had been hung. A patrolman directed Paavo to the side room where a group had gathered.

He led Angie to the room. "Wait here while I talk to Rebecca and Bill Sutter about what we're dealing with."

She nodded.

As soon as she was seated, he left her to get a feel for the area of Tardis Hall not cordoned off by yellow tape. The building was huge. Apart from that which had been turned into a lecture hall, the rest of it had been a warehouse with open space in the center, metal stairs and catwalks two or more stories high, and storage rooms on the sides.

"Paavo!" The medical examiner, Evelyn Ramirez, called out to him as she approached. Even at this time of night, every hair was in place, her makeup flawless. "I've already informed Rebecca and Bill that I'm not going out on that skylight, in the dark, on a roof slick from rain. I'll do my check of the body once it's brought indoors. I'm waiting for the photographer—who is out there—to take all the photos necessary for you guys."

"This isn't my case, Doc," he said. "I just decided to drop in."

"It's not another one, is it?" She drew a deep breath and gave a little shudder. "I understand there were a bunch of UFO wackos here tonight, and I know they're into cattle mutilations—much like what we saw with the last two bodies. Do you think there's any connection?"

"I don't know yet." Paavo was surprised to see the tough lady examiner squeamish about anything. "From what I've been told, this one was *only* splattered all over a skylight in the bathroom," he added with heavy sarcasm.

"And me without a ladder." She stomped off to see what the delay was at getting the body where she could examine it.

Paavo watched her go. He really shouldn't follow since it wasn't his case, and he knew how furious he got when other inspectors trampled through his crime scene out of curiosity. Not being able to see the crime galled, nonetheless. He turned and studied the three men seated in the side room with Angie. All of them, whether they knew it or not, were suspects. One by one, each would give Rebecca and Bill Sutter the particulars about who they were, where they lived and worked, and why they were there.

Three people.

Paavo walked closer to them. One looked like a thirty-something college professor, lacking only suede patches on the elbows of his sports jacket. Another had long, stringy blond hair pulled back in a ponytail; his clothes looked even dirtier than his hair. The last could have been a choirboy—white shirt, light gray slacks and solid blue tie.

The college professor type stood up and left the room to approach him. Paavo waited. "Excuse me, but you seem to be a friend of Angelina's," the fellow said. He looked nervous and his voice was shaky.

"I am." Paavo eyed him. Was that line an attempt on a suspect's part to ingratiate himself, or what?

The man rubbed his hands nervously. "With the police, are you?"

Paavo flipped open his badge, watching the man's every move. "Smith, Homicide."

The man read it over. "I'm, uh, I'm Derrick Holton, president of the club that put on the lecture tonight," he said, then held out his hand. Paavo shook it. "Angelina's a great woman." He spoke quickly, his eyes nervously darting from side to side. "We're old friends, you know."

"Is that so?" Paavo said, keeping his voice and expression emotionless.

"Ah, yes! Good friends." Derrick smiled again and looked back at Inspector Mayfield who was talking to the grubby blond fellow. His smile disappeared when he again faced Paavo. "That's why she came here tonight. To see me." He was growing breathless. "She's interested in UFO's, you know."

Paavo's eyes narrowed as he wondered if this pile of nerves was the guy Stan had told him about. "I didn't know that."

Derrick gave a high-pitched chuckle. "That was why she called me. Because of my background in the field." He slid his hands in his front trouser pockets and leaned forward. "So, since we're all friends of Angelina's, maybe you can get them to cut us some slack, you know? It's not as if any one of us would hurt Oliver. They're saying they might keep us here for hours. This... this isn't a great part of the city this late at night. It's dangerous, as I'm sure you know. Can you do anything to speed this up? I-I'd like to see that Angelina gets home safely."

Paavo took out his notebook, not trusting himself to speak right then, and made an annotation. "So, you know Miss Amalfi pretty well, do you?"

Derrick's smile broadened even more. "Yes," he murmured, then teetered back on his heels. "You could say that. We were close. Nearly got married."

Paavo felt as if he'd been sucker punched. Angie had never told him she'd been engaged. "Really?"

"That's right." Derrick nodded. He seemed much less nervous as the talk turned to Angie. A secret smile suddenly formed on his lips, giving Paavo the urge to ram a fist into the guy's face. "She was too young, though," Derrick finally announced. "She had things to do. She went off and lived in Paris for a while, traveled. I've never been far away, though. I promised to wait for her, and I did. Never really met anyone else quite like Angelina—a delightful mixture of vivacious earthiness and delicacy."

"Delightful, is she?" Paavo's jaw grew so tight he could barely pry his lips apart to speak.

"Oh, yes! Now, I just need to convince her the time is right for our wedding. Why wait?"

"Why indeed?" Paavo muttered.

"I can always call her old man and enlist his support now that Angelina and I are seeing each other again."

A chill raced through Paavo's veins. "Her father approves of you?" He didn't really need to ask. He was being masochistic. It was obvious from Derrick's words what the answer would be. Sal Amalfi had never thought a cop was good enough for his daughter.

"Her father and I"—Derrick pressed two fingers close together—"are just like that."

Paavo had to change the subject. "You live and work in the city, I take it?"

"I'm teaching at the UC Berkeley campus. Say, can't we talk tomorrow? Can't you tell them to release us?"

"So, you're a professor there?"

Derrick frowned impatiently. "Actually, I'm an astrophysicist. I spend more time on research than teaching. I was with NASA." He gave a smile probably meant to look self-deprecating. In fact, it looked anything but. "I guess I should have introduced myself more properly as *Doctor* Derrick Holton, Ph.D."

"Right." Paavo tried to hide the sneer in his voice. "And now that Miss Amalfi is interested in UFOs, she called you?"

"That's right. For her new job."

Christ! For her job? She told this guy about her new job as well? "Oh?" He struggled to keep his tone light and casual.

Derrick smiled and shook his head. "Sorry. I was beating myself up over there when I first saw you and Angelina together. I assumed there might be something between you two. I see I was wrong." He looked heavenward. "Thank you, Lord. Angelina has a business catering dinner parties for rich clients. It's quite successful, I understand. Plus, it's fun, and she enjoys it. I would have thought she would have told more people about it, but I guess she's only telling those she's close to."

Paavo felt as if someone could push him over with a feather. Was Angie lying to him or to this ... this astrophysicist? "People like you, in other words?"

"Yeah. Me. Connie. Earl at the restaurant."

His head was swimming now, his voice low. "So, you've been to Wings of An Angel?"

"Of course. It's one of Angelina's favorite spots."

"So I've heard." Paavo took a long, hard look at the man in front of him. "That's all very interesting, Mr. Holton. Or, I guess I should say, *Doctor* Holton."

"Whatever. And, yes, I thought you'd agree."

"I do. But it doesn't have anything to do with the reason we're here tonight, does it?"

Derrick's eyes widened. "Not directly, but I wanted to explain my character, my friends, my —"

"Whereabouts, *Doctor* Holton? I'm interested in your

whereabouts this evening, specifically from the time this 'Oliver Hardy' person was last seen alive, up until *Miss* Amalfi found his body."

Derrick stiffened. "Surely, you aren't implying that I..." As his eyes searched Paavo's face, he stopped talking and swallowed so hard his Adam's apple looked ready to spring from his throat.

Paavo's voice turned icy. "I'm not implying anything, Holton. Inspector Mayfield will be questioning you soon."

Derrick's mouth dropped open, and he visibly shuddered.

Paavo turned away and went to Angie.

She stood up, eyes wide as she studied his expression. "Paavo, what's wrong?"

"Put your coat on. I'll see that you get back safely to your apartment."

"You'll what?" Her face was filled with confusion.

Rebecca came running over to him. "Did I hear you say you're leaving? You can't take my witness until I say so."

"Have you gotten her statement?"

"A preliminary one, yes," Rebecca said.

"Then you know where to find her if you want more information later. And check out Derrick Holton real close. I don't like his attitude."

He grabbed Angie's arm and nearly lifted her from her shoes as he strode out the door.

Angie drove to her apartment building with Paavo following in his Mustang. When they reached her parking garage, she made sure the door stayed open so he could pull in. He parked in what would have been Stan Bonnette's spot, if Stan had a car.

They rode up in the elevator in silence. She glanced at Paavo, but he wouldn't meet her eyes. His mouth and teeth were shut so tight the jaws of life probably couldn't get them apart. Angie tried a few pleasantries, but he didn't answer.

She unlocked the door to her apartment. As soon as they stepped inside, she faced him.

"Why are you so angry with me?" she asked innocently. "I guess I shouldn't have phoned you, shouldn't have gotten you involved, but—"

"What the hell's going on, Angie?" His voice was harsh, his eyes fierce.

His question confused her. "With Oliver Hardy's death?"

"With you!" he bellowed.

Her breathing quickened. Why was he so angry? Her own anger flared as she took off her coat and opened the closet door to hang it up. "I have no idea what you're talking about, or why you're shouting. But I don't like it one bit!"

"You don't like it?" His tone was deceptively soft. She braced herself. "You're right. I guess I should just say congratulations and get out of here." He turned toward the door.

"What congratulations?"

His eyes narrowed. "Your old fiancé told me he's seeing you again. And that he plans to marry you, *with* your father's blessing."

His words hung in the air. She felt as if all the blood drained from her body. She froze, her coat in one hand, a hanger in the other. "Derrick said that to you?"

"That's not all he said." Paavo strode toward her, one hand against the wall next to the closet.

She faced him, but backed up right into a row of coats and jackets. And then she saw the hurt in his eyes.

Paavo continued. "He said you've gotten a new business, a successful new business, that he's met Connie and Earl, and he's eaten at Wings of an Angel with you. I can't imagine all that has taken place in a few days' time, so you must've been seeing him while you're seeing me. *Were you ever going to tell me about him?*"

Heart pounding, she hung up her coat, struggling to keep her emotions in check, and then she faced him. "Do you honestly think I care so little about you I'm calling up old boyfriends to see if they're any better the second time around?" Fury, hurt, and disappointment hit all at once and she flung her arms out wide. "My God, Paavo, is that really how you see me? The fact is, Derrick was not my fiancé and I've never been engaged. I never met anyone I wanted to spend my life with until"—she turned away, not able to look at him—"until recently. Happy, now?"

He stepped toward her. "Angie, stop."

Tears filled her eyes. She walked closer to the window before she faced him again. "I only wanted to do something that would make my family *and you* proud of me. Instead, it's all gone to hell."

"Ang—"

"Just listen, please!" She folded her arms. "I'll explain once, and then I want you to leave." She then gave him a quick rundown of her Fantasy Dinners idea and of Triana Criswell hiring her to put on a dinner about UFOs and space aliens, which led to her contacting Derrick Holton. She introduced Derrick to Connie, hoping the two of them would hit it off.

"Instead of anything good coming of all this," she said, "Dr. Mosshad has disappeared, Oliver is dead, Derrick seems to believe in this alien nonsense, Connie is going to be mad when I talk to her about ditching Derrick, and now you hate me. It turns out that no matter what I try to do, something screws it up. So, now you know. You can leave."

She started toward her bedroom, but he grabbed her wrist, stopping her.

"Don't you know I've always been proud of you?" he said.

She pulled her wrist free. "Well, you've got a hell of a way to show it."

"I don't give a damn about your business success or lack of it! Some of the most successful businessmen and women around are the worst assholes you could imagine."

She felt as if steam should shoot out of her ears. "And that's supposed to make me feel better? Go!"

"But Angie—"

"Just go! Leave! Now!"

He opened the door and stepped out to the hallway. "We'll talk tomorrow, okay?"

She shut the door on him without answering. Then, she shut her eyes and leaned her forehead against it.

As Paavo's words of his meeting with Derrick came back to her, she could just imagine Derrick lording his degree and his background over Paavo. She would never forgive Derrick for doing that.

The intensity of Paavo's reaction to all Derrick had implied about their relationship told her how much he'd been hurt by what he'd heard. But then, for Paavo to believe she could get over how she felt about him so quickly hurt her badly.

It was as if he didn't take her feelings about him seriously.

The realization that he simply didn't trust her enough made her eyes fill with tears again.

14

"How's the investigation going, Rebecca?" Paavo asked as he took the chair beside Inspector Mayfield's desk the next afternoon when she returned from Oliver Hardy's autopsy.

She looked over at him and smiled. "Well, hello." The other inspectors loved to point out to him that the only time Rebecca let down her I'm-as-tough-a-cop-as-any-man stance was when she was around him. "I don't think there's anything here that warrants much more looking into. Seems fairly cut and dried, actually."

"How so?" he asked.

"It's as Sutter and I concluded last night. Harding—his real name is John Oliver Harding—was depressed about his mother's death. The two had been close, and her death devastated him. He had no other relatives, no friends to speak of, and he was weird, clumsy, and overweight. He was not only into UFOs, but a fanatic about the 'coming Armageddon' and that the world was going to end soon. His only job was getting people to sign up for membership with the NAUTS—the National Association of Ufological Technology Scientists, offering a hundred-dollar sweepstakes. But we never did find any list that anyone ever won the sweepstakes."

"It figures." Paavo's mouth downturned.

"He apparently thought life was meaningless. You're born, you suffer, you die. In other words, a prime candidate for crawling out on a window ledge and just letting go."

"Nice psychology, Rebecca. Now let's hear it by the book."

She shrugged. "There are no police procedures for this. He died from the fall—that's what the autopsy concluded. We'll wait for the toxicology reports. Maybe he was high or drunk. Apparently he was no stranger to marijuana, and even a little crack now and then. He might have gone there to toke up."

"You would have found evidence."

"We might still."

"If you keep looking, yes."

Rebecca tightened her lips. "I know, I know. We will keep looking. No conclusions, yet."

Paavo nodded. "One other thing, what have you learned about Derrick Holton? He claims to have been a scientist with NASA. Is that true?"

"Not only is it true, apparently he was one of the brightest they had. Then for 'a change of scenery' some five years ago, he asked for a temporary transfer. They sent him off to a facility in Nevada. It changed him. He said that once there, he could no longer work at a place he had lost trust in. He quit NASA and became president of a UFO group called the NAUTS, as in astro*nauts*."

Paavo remembered Holton saying Angie left him to go to Paris, and he knew she was there some five years ago. He wondered if the breakup was what drove Holton from the Bay Area. But what could have happened in Nevada to change him so much he turned away from his profession?

"Did you ask him why he felt that way about NASA?"

"I tried, but I couldn't get any answers that made sense."

"What were his answers?"

"He kept repeating that he could no longer be a part of a lie, not after he had seen the truth. But he wouldn't say what the truth was, only that I wouldn't understand."

Paavo shook his head, also not knowing what Derrick meant. Soon, Rebecca left and Paavo went back to his desk.

"What's up, partner?" Yosh asked, lifting his head from the report he was writing about their continued lack of findings on Felix Rolfe's murder. "I can see the wheels turning full speed in that brain of yours."

"It's nothing," he said.

"Oh? You could have fooled me. Everything okay with Angie?"

"Angie? What makes you ask?"

"I guess women are on my mind." He turned back to his report. "It's nothing."

"Women?" Paavo asked. "Why is that?"

"Nothing."

Paavo sat down at his desk, swiveled his chair toward Yosh and leaned back. He remembered an odd reaction Yosh had a few days back to one of Inspector Calderon's typical caustic comments about relationships. Calderon sometimes sounded like a walking sexist, but Paavo knew he was going through a tough divorce, and tended to take it out on everyone.

"We've been partners long enough, Yosh," he said after a while, "that I've learned we both say it's nothing when it's something. Want to tell me what's going on?"

Yosh snapped his head toward Paavo, surprise etched on his face. "You trying to tell me you can see behind my 'mysterious-East' facade? And everyone in the bureau says *you're* the most inscrutable SOB they've ever met. What does this mean? Are we learning how to read each other?"

Paavo grinned. "Looks like."

Yosh tossed aside his pen and leaned back in his chair. "The thing is, I should be feeling really good about Nancy. She's developed an interest in calligraphy—the writing of stylized Chinese characters."

"Your wife is studying Chinese? That's interesting."

"Not the language, just how to write it. It's a kind of art. We call them *kanji* in Japanese. An entire painting might consist of just one character—say, love, or trust, or tree. The painter tries to make the *kanji* somehow evoke the feeling of the word. There's a lot of skill, too, that goes into the brush strokes used. The artist can't let his hand shake or use more than one brushstroke to make each line of the *kanji*. Each line must be perfect."

"It sounds pretty difficult."

"It is. She's apparently very good at it. She goes to class all the time. Her teacher, her *sensei*, as she calls him, encourages her."

"I don't get it," Paavo said. "What's the problem?"

Yosh took a deep breath before he continued. "Lately, she's been working on the word center. Center. Sounds simple, right? While she works, she has to think about the deep meaning of the word. About what's at *her* center, and what's at the center of our marriage. Of me!" He stopped speaking, his expression pained.

"There's plenty at your center," Paavo said. "Your ethics, for starters, and your heart, and your empathy despite the world you deal with. Nancy knows all that."

"Not well enough," he said quietly.

"She needs to hang around the people we have to face every day. Talk about people with no center," Paavo said quietly as his thoughts turned to Angie, how she had centered him and seemed to have become the heart of everything he thought of, dreamed of, even believed in—which, although he believed it was right not to see her anymore, was also why he had felt so devastated at everything Derrick Holton had told him. He glanced up at Yosh. "Nancy should look at the people involved with all these crazy UFO cults. For all their so-called searching, most have no idea what to believe, or where the truth is. They find truth in nothing, and as a result, they believe anything. Where is their center?"

"Nancy compared me and my center with her *sensei*," Yosh said. "I came up short. Actually, I came up tall. He's a squirrelly little guy—small, refined, like upper-class Japanese. Me, I'm big. Northern Japanese peasant stock. Not very exciting stuff."

"I can't believe it," Paavo said. "Nancy's crazy about you."

"She used to be. Now, she's turning back to other things Japanese. Calligraphy. The tea ceremony with all its stylized gentleness. This *sensei* encourages her in that, too. She's even taking Japanese lessons! Being third generation, like I am, she never learned to speak the old language, just a word here and there. But with all this diversity stuff being so big here in the city, she's thinking that if everyone else in the country sees her as Japanese first and American second, she may as well study what it's all about."

"That has nothing to do with your relationship."

"I don't know. What's more Japanese?" Yosh studied the floor. "An artistic teacher or a cop who studies dead bodies. A man who looks for a mutilation murderer isn't the sort my wife finds thrilling these days."

Paavo's shoulders slumped. "I know what you mean," he said wearily. "Angie's got an old boyfriend hanging around her. She says she's not interested in him, but the guy is still plenty interested in her. He told me so."

Yosh's head lifted. "You're kidding."

"He told me her father approves of him."

"Shit."

"And he's got a Ph.D."

Yosh smacked his fist on the desktop. "Hell, does he walk on water, too?"

"He believes in UFOs."

Yosh's mouth dropped open, then he began to chuckle. "Now you're talking."

Paavo stared out the window. "It's easy to catch onto that one quirk and overlook what makes the guy good for a woman like Angie."

"You're good for a woman like Angie, pal." Yosh was exuberant, sounding like his upbeat self again. "She knows it and so do I. I wouldn't throw you over for some scientific geek."

Paavo grinned. "That's good to hear. And if I was Nancy, I wouldn't throw you over for some scrawny painter."

Yosh laughed. "Why don't women have the good sense we do?"

"Damned if I know."

Yosh thought a moment. "You know, maybe I should get Nancy this vacuum cleaner she's been talking about wanting. I could even surprise her with it. A nice gift!"

Paavo shook his head, his eyes mischievous. "You do that, Yosh, and you're going to make that painter look better than ever."

The two were still chuckling about that when Paavo got a call from Faldo in CSI. "Good news, that disk you found on your vice is a prototype of an early integrated circuit chip. It had a number stamped in that I was able to look up. It was last in the hands of someone named Neumann, and when he died, some ten years ago, it was shown as transferred to someone called Algernon. One name only.

"But that's not all," Faldo added. "There was a good fingerprint on it—most likely Algernon's—and it matched the partial we found on the night vision goggles. So we strongly suspect Algernon's real name is Myron Ramsbottom."

Angie felt like a zombie when she walked into The Wings of An Angel just before noon. Earl hurried her to a table. "What can I get you to drink, Miss Angie? You aren't lookin' so hot today."

"Gee, thanks, Earl. I really needed to hear that." She put her head in her hands. "Just some coffee."

"You wanna sangwich? Some spaghetti?"

"I'll have something light—how about a frittata?"

"I don' t'ink Butch has much fancy stuff to put in one—no aspary-gus or any a dat kinda stuff."

"Diced onions, a little cheese, plus ham or Italian sausage would be great."

"Oh. I t'ink he can do dat." Earl's eyebrows scrunched with worry. "So, how's da inspector dese days?"

She glanced up at him. "I hope he's okay," she admitted. She couldn't stop thinking about their words last night. His feelings—good and bad—ran deep. The realization that she'd hurt him, disappointed him, although she hadn't meant to, had her feeling miserable.

Earl's gaze held hers a moment, his eyes sad, then he gave a small nod and walked back toward the kitchen. Angie slumped back in her chair. Most of last night seemed like a bad dream. She'd fallen asleep watching a lecture, and from that time on, everything that happened seemed out of focus.

Earl soon returned with a tall, steaming cup of coffee and placed it before her. "Butch'll make you a real good frittata, Miss Angie. His cookin'll make you feel a lot better."

"Thanks, Earl."

The door to the restaurant opened, and two of Earl's favorite customers, Rose and Lena, entered. Earl slicked back his hair, straightened his spine, and strutted over to welcome them. He was obviously sweet on them both.

As Angie sipped her coffee, her mind replayed the horrible scene last night at the lecture hall. Why would Oliver Hardy have committed suicide? Or, if not that, why would anyone want to kill him? Personally, she had found him too strange for words, but the others didn't seem bothered by him.

She tried to turn her thoughts to the Fantasy Dinner, tried to plan some menus, but images of Tardis Hall and Paavo's unhappiness got in the way.

Just then, Vinnie came through the kitchen doors, marched straight to Angie's table, pulled out a chair and sat down. Vinnie, like Earl, was somewhere in his sixties, but where Earl was short and round and solid having once worked as a bouncer in Vegas, Vinnie was short and round and soft. Probably because his chief form of work was to order Butch, the restaurant's cook, or Earl to do something. Angie was surprised to see him, though. He rarely ventured out of his downstairs office.

"I heard that you're actin' real down," he said. All three of the guys had similar old-time San Francisco accents, which was an offshoot of the New Yorkers and Irish who had settled in the city over a century earlier.

"Yeah. I tried to start a new business," she began. "Big mistake."

With a hangdog look, he slowly nodded. "That'll make a person miserable real fast."

"I'm supposed to cater a big meal for a strange group of people, and I've got to do it in a week's time. I've been calling around for caterers, and they all act like I'm crazy. If I keep the job, I'll have to prepare all the food myself."

"Oh, yeah? How many people you talkin' about?"

"I don't know."

"What're you gonna serve 'em?"

"I haven't decided."

"You got a problem all right. Maybe you oughta serve 'em chips an' dip."

"Maybe I should just give up."

He leaned forward. "You ain't no quitter, Miss Angie. An' if this is so important to you, me an' the boys'll help you."

She glanced up at him. "You will?"

"Sure. You gotta remember, we don' do nothin' fancy. But we can get people fed."

"Thanks, Vinnie. I appreciate it."

He sat back, relaxed, his wrinkled face curving into a smile. "Hey, you helped us get this restaurant goin'. We couldn'a done it without you. It's payback time, that's all."

"I don't need any payback. But I'm glad of your offer."

"An' anyway, we gotta keep an eye on you an' see that you don' get no more sad or mixed up about stuff than you are."

As Angie's heart swelled at his insightful words, he got up, pushed in the chair and went back into the nether regions of the restaurant to do whatever it was he usually did. Which, she suspected, wasn't much.

15

"Damn it to hell," Yosh bellowed. "We've got to get that bastard. I mean, now. Right now!" Thick fog swirled around him like smoke from a fire blotting out the rest of the city. It was early morning, and the little party that stood at the top of the southernmost peak of Twin Peaks seemed to be the only people left on earth.

Paavo pulled his jacket tighter to ward off the damp cold. Another mutilation murder, every bit as horrible as the last two, had been committed. The body was that of an African-American male, probably in his mid-to-late fifties, although guessing the age of someone who had been exsanguinated wasn't easy. The skin tended to turn as dry and flaky as that of a ninety-year-old. Like the other two victims, he was naked, bloodless, and his entire abdominal area had been cored out. Like the other two, he had a number carved in his chest. This time, the number was four. Only one thing was different. Wrapped around the victim's wrist was a piece of cable.

The man had been left on the open ground—an area few people climbed up to, preferring the paved drive for sightseeing, or the north peak if they were in the mood to climb.

An early-morning dog walker had to chase his dog up there and then found the body.

Between the nearly constant rain and fog, he had missed walking his dog the last few days.

The dog walker had been held until the homicide inspectors could talk to him.

"The body looks like he's been out here a couple of days," Paavo said to Yosh.

"Felix Rolfe was freshly killed when we found him just four days ago," Yosh said. "We've got a real psycho on our hands. He doesn't seem to get physically tired or emotionally drained from these killings."

"And, why is there a four carved on his chest? Seven, five, four," Paavo said.

"We need a break!" Yosh muttered. "Some prints on this vic, something. The doer's got to make a mistake soon. These killings are too bloody for there not to be any evidence!"

"Maybe three's the charm." Paavo scanned the eerie crime scene of another horrible, senseless murder.

There were no houses at the very top of Twin Peaks, but those nearby held prospective witnesses who had to be interviewed. Paavo had planned, before this, to spend the day tracking down the Algernon character whose prints were on the weird items left at crime scenes. Instead, he and Yosh would need to follow the routine for identifying yet another mutilated corpse.

The only good thing about these horrible murders and the twenty-four-seven time he needed to put in to catch whoever was doing them, meant he couldn't dwell on Angie and how much she had once meant to him. He drew in a deep breath and said to Yosh, "Let's get started."

Paavo spent all the rest of that morning working the newest crime scene as well as trying to find some clue from the prior two as to exactly what was going on in the city.

He brought the cable to Faldo in CSI. Faldo immediately turned to prototypes with this latest object. The cable turned out to be a prototype of a fiber optic cable.

Paavo had just returned to his desk when his desk phone rang. "Smith, here."

"Sergeant Cooper, Park station. Some of my men heard about the body up on the Peaks. They told me about a woman looking for her husband. She'd called the past two nights, checking jails, hospitals, and accident reports. Now, my guys think the husband might fit the description of your corpse." He proceeded to give Paavo the contact information.

"Damn," Paavo muttered after he hung up the phone. It was bad enough talking to cold or heartless people like Bertram Lambert's sister or Felix Rolfe's mother about a loved one being killed. To talk to a victim's wife was the worst part of his job.

Paavo and Yosh went to a walkup flat on Broderick near Waller. "Mrs. Cole?" Paavo asked when a tall middle-aged African-American woman opened the door.

She was in her bathrobe and slippers. One look at the men in front of her and she stiffened, her face etched with worry and fright. "That's me. It's about Leon, isn't it? Did you find him? Is he hurt?" Her voice held the soft cadence of the South.

"We're checking on your call that he's missing, Mrs. Cole," Yosh said gently, as he and Paavo pulled out their IDs. "I'm Inspector Yoshiwara and this is Inspector Smith."

"Inspectors?" she asked, her dark brown eyes growing wider, as if wondering why her call had attracted such high-level attention. But then her shoulders slumped with the realization of what might be the reason.

"Yes, ma'am," Yosh continued. "Do you have any pictures of your husband? That would help us."

That seemed to rattle her. "A picture?" she said, backing away from the door. "Come in," she murmured as she went into the living room. A gallery of photographs—young boys, smiling girls, toothless kids, all ages and sizes, lined the mantle over what had once been a fireplace, but now had a gas heater in it.

"These are our kids and grandkids," she said proudly. "Our kids are all grown up. It's just me and Leon at home now." She picked up a photo of a military man wearing an Air Force uniform. Paavo and Yosh immediately glanced at each other, recognizing him as the man they had found on the street. "This photo is a few years old—his retirement from the Air Force after twenty-five years of service. He was a captain. He hasn't changed too much, though. Still a handsome rascal. Does this help?"

"Yes, it's a big help," Yosh said, in his warm, friendly manner. "Thank you."

Paavo and Yosh glanced at each other, then asked her to sit down. She would have to, eventually, go down to the morgue with them. But not right now.

16

That evening, Angie went into her living room, turned on the TV, kicked off her black four-inch heel Ferragamos and flopped onto the sofa, exhausted.

She had hoped Paavo would stop by to talk after their argument and the way she'd ordered him to leave. He always had in the past when things were strained between them, although this time, it was a lot more than a "strain." But then she heard on the news that another mutilated body had been found, so she knew how busy he had to be between reporters, his bosses, and City Hall demanding he and Yosh find the killer or killers immediately.

Still, the way they'd parted caused her to feel as if a part of her was missing, as if there was an emptiness where her heart had once been.

Now, after a simple dinner, she settled down to watch *Cooking for Fun and Profit* when the buzzer sounded on her door.

She spun around and faced it with surprise. Paavo never used the doorbell. He always knocked. So did Stan. She put her shoes back on, went to the peephole and peered out.

Then she swung open the door. "Derrick! This is a surprise."

"Angie." He stood in the doorway, his eyes shifting and fearful. "I wanted to be sure everything was all right with you. Everyone is so upset about Oliver, I scarcely know what to do."

"I can imagine. Come in."

"Thank you. I didn't want to impose." He glanced over his shoulder toward the elevator then hurriedly stepped into her living room and shut the door behind him. He drew in a deep breath as he looked around. "This apartment is even more beautiful than I remember." He headed toward the windows and peeked behind an open drape. Angie watched him with growing discomfort. "Your father owns a gold mine with this building," he said. "Top of Russian Hill. Views. He hasn't given it to you, has he?"

What was with him, Angie wondered. "I don't think my four sisters would like it if he did." She gestured toward the sofa. "Won't you sit down? How about some brandy or scotch?"

"Brandy would be great. It's chilly out. The fog is thick again tonight. The airports are closed. Traffic is scarcely moving."

"Yes. I was out earlier." She poured him a snifter of brandy. He took off his jacket and sat. She sat on the antique yellow Hepplewhite chair.

"So..." She was tempted to talk to him about his conversation with Paavo and how unhappy she was with him, but then she decided her emotions were still too raw, and she was simply too tired to listen to his excuses or comments about it. "How are you holding up after all this?"

"It's hard." His gaze dropped a moment. "More than anything, I'm numb right now. First Mosshad, now Oliver. Poor Oliver. Heaven forbid Mosshad is also dead. Still, I'm afraid something terrible has happened to him. And now, three mutilation murders. I've never heard of such things performed on humans! I'm scared, Angie, and I'm not too much of a man to admit it."

"Derrick," she wasn't quite sure how to bring this up, "tell me the truth. Wasn't Mosshad's disappearance a publicity stunt? I mean, none of you sounded sincerely upset when it happened."

As he held the snifter he slowly turned it, his thumb running along the side of the glass as he did. "Of course it was a publicity stunt. It was supposed to be over in two days and give everyone a good laugh, that's all. It was a way to get the public's attention. The NAUTS is barely viable, I'm sorry to say. It seems we aren't 'far out' enough. If we had one hundredth of the money that charlatan Algernon is raking in, we'd be fine. But we don't."

"You called Algernon a charlatan, but you faked the abduction."

"We would have admitted it was a joke, and after we'd gotten some attention, we would explain that. But everything else we were involved in is very, very real."

"I don't understand how you did it. I was there. And even I believed I'd lost time until I left and discovered my watch was correct."

"It was just a trick, Angie, and not that difficult. We're scientists and engineers. We have access to all kinds of things and the know-how to use them. We had the chairs in the audience rigged up to make quick, strong, electro-magnetic charges in the armrests. When we hit a switch, the charges were released. They actually did make a few watch batteries stop. The big clocks in the hall all run off a master clock. Using the master, we moved them ahead ten minutes. The result was simple. Once a few people began shouting that they'd lost ten minutes, that was all it took to convince the bulk of the audience. To lose time is a common phenomenon in abductions. By the time they left the hall and saw clocks with the real time, like you did, who knows what they thought? I'm sure a number of them got the joke and laughed it off."

"That's remarkable," Angie said, thinking a lot of people wouldn't laugh, and probably would never trust the NAUTS again.

"Anyway, my announcement that Mosshad had been abducted made the newspapers. We planned his return so that anyone who wanted more information could attend his lecture."

"What a scam!" she cried.

"Not a scam, a stunt, and a mild one, believe me," Derrick said with a shrug. "There was just one problem. Mosshad never made his grand return."

"Are you sure he isn't simply hiding somewhere, letting the suspense build?"

"I doubt it. He needed to reappear before the public forgot the story—a couple of days max. I think something has happened to him."

"Did you go to the police?" Angie asked.

"And say what? We told a guy to get lost for a couple of days and he hasn't come back yet?"

"Exactly."

"How much attention will the police give us when they find out we're all NAUTS?"

Remove the 'A,' Angie thought, but said, "You may have a point."

"I'm scared," Derrick admitted. "We were wrong to pretend he was abducted. I, of all people, should know better than to play around with that since... No, forget it."

"Forget what?" She asked eyeing him with caution.

He shook his head. "You won't believe me."

"Try me, at least," she offered.

He took a deep breath, then blurted out, "I believe I've been abducted several times. It happens at night, while I'm asleep. I've woken up in strange places, usually in my car!"

She stared at him, weighing a variety of comments in her head. She finally settled on, "Are you sure you aren't sleep-walking?"

He looked offended at her suggestion. "It's far too real to be a dream!"

"What did you see or do while abducted?" she asked.

"I don't know. I can't remember. Perhaps thankfully."

"You remember nothing at all?"

"Nothing!" He practically shouted the word. Still clearly agitated, he continued. "Enough about all that. The more important issue is, I don't believe Oliver killed himself. He had no reason to! I'm afraid someone, or something, is after the NAUTS. And as president of the group, that puts me in danger!" Embarrassed at his outburst, he turned his head away, and began rubbing his temples. "Between the abduction and Oliver, I'm afraid to go back to my apartment, to be alone."

She knew what he was asking, but there was no way she was about to invite him to stay at her place. "Maybe you could stay with one of the NAUTS?"

He sighed. "I don't think so." He then drained his glass and looked at her with puppy dog eyes. She remembered that look when they were dating, as if it was up to her to "make things right." She didn't like it then, and liked it even less now. "I'll figure something out," he whispered. "I shouldn't have bothered you."

"Wait. Before you leave, we should call Paavo. Maybe he can suggest something to help find Mosshad. He might know, as well, if Oliver's death was an accident or suicide. Perhaps you don't need to be fearful about any of this."

"No. Don't call him. It'll work out, in time. For now, I need to decide what to do. It's not your problem." As he studied her, his hazel eyes seemed wary and strained in a way that didn't fit her old friend at all. Then, to her horror, his face started to crumble, and she thought he was going to burst into tears. He swallowed hard a few times, looking like an inflatable doll that just had a pin stuck into it, and then sank back onto the sofa. "It's just so hard." He blinked away tears and then gazed at her. "You're the only person left in this whole world that I trust."

He was making her more and more uncomfortable. "Me? What about your NAUTS friends?"

He sighed and shut his eyes a moment. "What if one of them is behind this? What if one of them has...has hurt Mosshad, or was behind Oliver's death, and now is after me?"

"You're leaping to all sorts of conclusions, Derrick."

"What if those conclusions are true?" His voice rose, and he seemed half hysterical. "Do I have to be the next one killed before anyone believes me? Angie, I hate to ask, but if I could just stay here a few days..."

She sat on the sofa beside him and took his hand. "You need to calm down. Look at me and tell me the truth. Is there some reason you believe you can't trust your friends? If I'm going to help you, I need to know."

His hand tightened painfully on hers. "I don't know who to trust. I believe some Prometheans have infiltrated the NAUTS. They hate that I'm making the NAUTS successful, to some extent."

"I don't follow," she said.

His lips tightened. "After you and I broke up, I went to Area 51 in Nevada, where the founder of the Prometheus Group, I.M. Neumann, had worked until he was killed some five years before I got there."

"Area 51?" she asked. "The secret government facility?"

"Right. It's near Groom Lake in Nevada. Also near Nellis Air Force Base. Lots of black budget experiments go on there. The military denies anything special happens in the complex. But I know better. While there, I learned about Neumann, his work, and the Prometheus Group. It was once a great group. But after Neumann's death—his lab blew up while he was in it—Algernon took it over. He perverted the group into the paranormal garbage, made it 'showy,' even posted videos on YouTube, for crying out loud. So, Frederick Mosshad, who knew I.M. Neumann, started the NAUTS because he hated the way Algernon had changed the Prometheus Group."

"The split was pretty ugly, I take it," Angie said.

"Absolutely. But Mosshad is old and weak, so the NAUTS posed no threat to the Promethean's until I got there. I met with the NAUTS and eventually they asked me to be president and moved Mosshad to the role of 'founder.' He's a great scientist, but not a group leader."

"What a mess," Angie said.

"It is."

Angie then asked, "What was the Prometheus' Group original cause?"

"It was to let the world know that aliens do exist, that they really did land on earth at Roswell, and that the government—despite its denials—not only knows they exist but has taken alien DNA and added it to a human embryo. And that a man walked among us, a brilliant man, who was in fact, half alien."

Oh, lordy, Angie thought, *here we go again.* She was almost afraid to ask her next question. "Who was that half alien, half man?"

"Who else? Igor Mikhailovich Neumann—I.M. Neumann, a man-alien combination." His eyes were wide, almost scary.

"Give me strength!" she cried, unable to take any more of this. "Igor Mikhailovich? That sounds Russian. Are you saying he was a half-Russian, half-space-alien creature?"

Derrick looked indignant at being questioned by a non-scientist. "It's well known that Russian defectors and ex-Nazi German scientists worked along with Americans for years after the Roswell crash on this project. Finally, sometime in the fifties, they succeeded, and I.M. Neumann was born—in a laboratory, of course, given his bizarre parentage."

"Ah, but of course. *I am new man.* How did I miss it?" It sounded like the sort of schmaltz Hollywood would come up with.

Derrick nodded. "That's right. And he was brilliant beyond human comprehension. From the time he was old enough to understand why he was so different from other children, he dedicated his life to learning all he could about science, both biophysics and astrophysics. He wanted to know everything; do everything he could about the sad state of denial the world was in."

"Denial?"

"About extraterrestrials. That they exist. Throughout his life he was watched and studied by the government, of course, and he worked at Area 51—almost a prisoner there. That was why, when his lab blew up, the government immediately moved in and let no one have access to anything. After all, what if his body was tested and found to have non-human DNA and word got out? Can you imagine what a stir that would cause? So, we have nothing left of him or his research."

Conspiracy Theory 101. "Derrick," Angie murmured, "what am I going to do with you?"

"It's true, Angie!" He walked over to the windows. "Please, believe me. At Area 51, I not only learned about Neumann, I saw the scientific basis for the alien landing at Roswell. I learned, to my horror, that our own government, even NASA, has been lying to us for years about UFOs and aliens. So, when I saw that Algernon had turned Neumann's life's work into touchy-feely, pyramid-loving nonsense, I was disgusted and said so publicly. Algernon has hated me ever since. Now there have been deaths. Horrible deaths. Oliver's. Maybe Mosshad's. Others."

"Others?" she asked, surprised.

"There might be." His eyes were hollow. "The mutilation murders." He clamped his mouth shut, his Adam's apple working as he seemed to swallow over and over. "The newspapers don't really tell what was done to the murder victims. From what I've read about these murders and about cattle mutilations, I can tell you, the patterns are similar. I think your detective friend won't be able to find who killed those men. He won't know where to look. He'll be looking for regular clues, normal methods. But these killers... these killers are not of this world!"

He worried her. As much is she wanted to get away from him, she also remembered the brilliant young scientist he had once been, and couldn't help but hope he might still exist somewhere under all this UFO madness. "I'll help you, Derrick," she said softly, cautiously. "I'll find a place for you to stay, somewhere you will feel safe. You've been under a strain. I hadn't realized how much of a strain..."

He folded his arms tight against himself as a shudder rippled through his body. "I shouldn't have troubled you with this."

"What are friends for?" She jumped up. "I'll talk to my neighbor across the hall. I'm sure he'll be able to help you. We'll just tell him you're new in the area and looking for an apartment. And we won't say anything to him about extraterrestrials."

Stan opened the hide-away bed in his living room. He didn't have a big apartment like Angie's. Only because of its small size, years of rent control, and his father's money, could he afford to live there. He didn't mind Angie's impressive astrophysicist friend staying with him a day or two. He might even have to call his workplace and say he had to stay home a few days to take care of a sick friend. That sounded downright noble.

"What are those?" Derrick asked, pointing at the two twisted pieces of aluminum foil on a lamp table.

"Nothing." Stan snatched them and crumbled them up. "I was just twirling some aluminum foil while watching TV."

"Oh. For a moment, there, they looked like something I've seen people do to protect themselves from strange waves in the air."

Halfway to the kitchen to throw the aluminum in the trash, Stan stopped. "Oh, really? You've heard of such things?"

"I have."

"And does it work?"

"I've heard it does. It's probably smart to protect oneself from all the radio waves and sonic beams floating around, let alone horrible transmissions from cell towers and windmills. And don't forget the chemtrails that airplanes spew out."

Stan's pulse quickened. He hadn't even considered those. "Do they all cause headaches?"

"Much worse than that. They can make your brain begin to deteriorate."

Stan turned pale as Derrick continued. "Think of it this way. Do any history books talk about Alzheimer's? No. Because it didn't exist before 1955 with the advent of television, when all these strange waves started smacking into our brains causing lesions. And at times, the electrical charges we're being hit with make our brains go haywire. Sort of like a short in a wire, if you know what I mean."

"I had no idea." Stan gulped hard. "Angie did say you're a NASA space scientist, right?"

"I was. I quit awhile back. NASA knows all this, but they don't want the public to know it. I was sick of hiding things."

"Wow. That's noble of you to give up that kind of job out of principal." Stan didn't know what to make of this guy. He didn't know anyone who acted that way. He backed out of the living room toward his bedroom. "Well, sleep tight. Let me know if there's anything I can do for you."

"I'll be fine. I really appreciate this," Derrick said as he sat down on the bed.

Stan rushed into his bedroom, took the aluminum pieces he'd crumbled and began reshaping them into cylinders as best he could and stuck them in his ears. Thoughts of shorted-out brains spurred him on. If NASA said wearing aluminum foil in the ears was a smart thing to do, that was good enough for him.

17

Angie waited until ten p.m. before arriving at Paavo's house. She could tell that the lights were on in the living room, although the blinds were shut, so she hoped she had guessed right by coming at this time. Any earlier, and he'd probably still be at work; later, and he might be asleep or so tired it would be difficult to talk to him. And she needed to.

She rang the doorbell, her heart pounding as she heard the deadlock snap back and the door open. He looked exhausted, his eyes too red, his face too pale. His shirt was untucked, and he wore old jeans and was barefoot. But to her, he looked delectable.

"Hi," she said.

His brow crossed. "What's this? Why are you here?"

"I learned something tonight that might—and I said might—have an effect on your investigations. I thought I should tell you about it."

He stared at her a while in that very cop-like way he had where she couldn't tell if he was ready to jump for joy or lock her up. Then he nodded. "Come on in."

His house, more a cottage or bungalow, was quite old and

small, one-bedroom, a huge eat-in kitchen, and a living room. But she loved it. It was homey and warm.

The front door led directly into the living room with its overstuffed, comfortable and mismatched sofa and easy chairs. Paavo's cat, Hercules, called Herk, lay on one of the chairs. He opened one eye, looked at her, yawned, stretched, and went back to sleep.

"I brought you some risotto and chicken," she said, handing him a plastic container. "You can zap it whenever you're hungry. I suspect you don't have much time to cook these days."

He took the container. "No, I don't. Thanks. This is thoughtful, but you didn't have to—"

"I know. I wanted to."

He stood awkwardly a moment. "I'll put it in the fridge. Want some coffee? Or beer?"

"No thanks. I'm fine." When he was out of the room, she removed her jacket and sat on one side of the sofa.

He returned to the living room, saw her, and sat on the sofa's opposite end. "You said you wanted to tell me about something."

She folded her hands on her lap. "I had a visit from Derrick Holton this evening." Paavo's jaw twitched the slightest bit. "He's scared."

That got a reaction. "Scared? Why?"

"He believes the mutilation murders, as the press calls them, has to do with someone, or perhaps several people, involved in these UFO groups. Now, he's afraid to stay in his own apartment, and is spending the night with Stan."

Paavo's eyebrows rose at this news. "Because John Oliver Harding was killed in Tardis Hall?"

"It's more than that," she explained. "Let me start from the beginning. It all has to do, apparently, with something that happened at a place called Roswell, and then Area 51, and a scientist called I. M. Neumann. I'm sorry I don't remember what the 'I' stood for. The 'M' was for Michailovich. He was part Russian and, supposedly, part alien."

Paavo's expression tightened. "Go on."

She went on to tell him everything Derrick had told her about the Promethean's and the NAUTS, and about their long-time feud, including Derrick's rivalry with Algernon.

Paavo listened with interest, not interrupting as she relayed Derrick's story. When she ended, his first question was puzzling.

"Did he mention the name Myron Ramsbottom?"

"Who?" she asked.

"Tell me about this Algernon. Have you ever seen him?"

"Of course. He's the guest of honor at my Fantasy Dinner, which, I'm sorry to say, has now morphed into my Nightmare Buffet."

Paavo shook his head. "I should have seen that coming. Tell me what he looks like, age and all."

He kept nodding as she gave age, build, and hair color. When she mentioned purple eyes, he asked, "Contacts?"

She nodded, then asked with a half-smile, "You aren't suggesting his real name is Myron Ramsbottom are you?"

"I am, especially since it seems he knew I. M. Neumann, so he might have touched some of the Roswell prototypes in Area 51—prototypes that... Well, that's not for distribution, okay?"

"I understand," she said. "But it sounds like you know something about Roswell?"

"Sure. I was fascinated by it when I was a kid."

"Can you tell me about it?"

He did a double-take. "You're kidding. You don't know about Roswell?"

"Not you, too!" Her lips downturned. "I've heard the name, but no details, okay?"

He grinned. "I guess it's more of a guy thing." He looked at her expectant expression. "Okay, it happened after the

Second World War in New Mexico—which also happens to be where the atomic bomb was developed. A lot of government secret stuff was always said to be going on out in the desert there."

"Okay," she murmured.

"One day, an object fell to earth just outside the tiny town of Roswell. The first military officer out there—Jesse Marcel was his name—said it was a flying saucer. And it made the local newspapers. Well, the big brass went crazy at that and came up with the story that it was only a weather balloon. Of course, very few people believed a high-ranking officer like Marcel, who'd been connected with Army intelligence, would mistake a weather balloon for a flying saucer. But for the most part, the story pretty much died for many years until the people involved got old and, I guess, decided they no longer much cared who didn't like what they had to say."

"Oh?" Angie listened intently.

"I guess it was in the 1980s or '90s that lot of stories about Roswell and what was really found there began to leak out. Marcel told his story, as did a guy who was a workman, a plumber or something, on the base, who said he saw four bodies being carried into a building on gurneys—and at least one of the bodies was still alive. But they weren't human."

"You're kidding!" Angie gasped. "And people believed his story?"

"You bet. Especially since he was backed up by others. Once a couple people began talking, it was like the floodgates opened. Some of the people who talked had been stationed near Roswell. Others were townspeople who said the military had threatened their lives if they said anything. They all swore what had landed in Roswell was no weather balloon, but came from outer space and had many things we've never had on earth. It's said that many of the tremendous technological leaps that happened in the 1950s and '60s were taken from the

Roswell crash site and had been reverse engineered by scientists."

"Really? What kinds of things?"

"Oh, let's see, it's hard to remember since it was years ago that I read this stuff. But there are still lots of books and online videos about it." Paavo took out his phone and googled Roswell and reverse engineering. "Here we go. Fiber optic cables, integrated circuit chips, lasers, Kevlar, and light amplification devices—which we call night vision glasses." He stopped talking a moment and gazed intently at his phone, and then he put the phone down. "Plus, a lot of other strange things that make no sense to me since they're so technical. Supposedly they also found a number of instruments whose functions we still don't understand."

"That's hard to believe," Angie said, surprised such nonsense was popular.

Paavo smiled at her reaction. "Most people scoff at the stories. On the other hand, some really brilliant people have worked on these things—men high up in the military and in Washington. An Army Lieutenant Colonel who had worked with General MacArthur as well as President Eisenhower wrote a bombshell book about Roswell and what he personally witnessed." She watched as a cloud seem to pass over his expression. "If you want details, I suspect an astrophysicist could tell you a lot more than I can."

She couldn't help but frown at that little dig. "Very funny, but you've told me quite enough."

He smirked. "In any case, Roswell now has gift shops filled with information, and even a UFO festival. The town has made quite a living out of these old stories."

"Well, that's quite the tale. So, what really landed in Roswell?"

"No one knows for sure. The most prevalent theory I've heard is that it was really some sort of top-secret experimental device the U.S. military was testing and that the bodies found were chimps. And that's why the military quickly clamped down on anything being said. But who knows?"

"I may have to read up on it," Angie said. "It's more interesting than I expected."

"Yes... very," he murmured, and then fell silent.

She waited, but when he said nothing more, she stood. "Well, I hope this information has been of some help. I'll be off now."

"It has." He walked her out to her car and even held the door as she got in. "Thank you, Angie."

She looked up at him a long moment, and then nodded. "Anytime, Inspector."

He shut the car door, in her rearview mirror she saw that he remained on the sidewalk, watching as she drove off."

18

"Angie! This is for you." Stan announced as he and Derrick stood in her doorway the next morning, each holding one end of a large box of Krispy Kreme doughnuts.

"Oh, my goodness!" she cried, accepting the box.

"We wanted to bring you something for breakfast, but not too much is open around here this early except some coffee places," Stan said.

"This is very thoughtful. Thank you." She liked a doughnut once in a blue moon, but a dozen? "Come in."

"We left my apartment," Stan said, "before we had breakfast."

Angie nodded. Now it all made sense. "I see. Did you sleep well, Derrick?"

"Yes, great. I appreciate you and Stan helping me out."

"I hate to mention this, Angie," Stan said, "but your hands have a greenish tint. You weren't slimed by an alien, were you?"

"It's food coloring," Angie said, distinctly unamused by his joke. "It's ruined my French manicure and I'm in no mood to discuss it."

"Ah, sounds like you're baking!" Stan sidled past her and headed for the kitchen.

"Is Stan right?" Derrick asked as he followed Stan.

"He is. I'm making little green space monster cookies."

"Oh, aren't they cute!" Stan cried as he saw an alien-shaped cookie cutter on the counter. He ogled the raw cookie dough. She picked up the rolling pin and used it to shoo Stan away. He could eat a bowl of raw cookie dough in no time flat.

"Tell you what," she said. "Let me put a batch of cookies in the oven, and then I'll make us all a nice brunch. And doughnuts will be our dessert."

"No hurry, Angie," Stan said with a smile. "We've got all day."

The doorbell rang.

"Now, who?" She wiped her hands and went to answer.

"Hi!" Connie stood in the doorway with a big bag from Athena's Greek Restaurant. "I was feeling bad that I wasn't there with you at Tardis Hall the other night. I thought I'd bring us lunch. Athena's serves a brunch, so I was able to get us some dolmas, moussaka and fides pilaf."

"Sounds wonderful. Come on in. Join the party."

"What party?" Connie said as she headed for the kitchen with the food. "How is your Fantasy Dinner coming—"

She stopped talking as she saw Derrick Holton standing by the sink. She gave him a big smile. "Derrick! What a surprise! What are you doing here?" But she no sooner asked the question, than her eyes opened wide and darted between Angie and Derrick. She gave Angie one of those "what-in-the-hell-is-going-on-and-why-didn't-you-tell-me-about-it-before-this?" looks.

Angie shook her head and rolled her eyes.

"I'm staying with Stan," Derrick said.

Connie hadn't even noticed Stan standing by the counter

eating green cookie dough. Her gaze bounced from him to Derrick, as if she couldn't imagine a more unlikely pair.

"And I'm getting ready for Algernon's party," Angie said, "which apparently is still going to happen."

"You're still holding a party for that fraud," Derrick grumbled.

"Why wouldn't she?" Connie said, helping her put the cut cookies onto a tray. "Why is the Cookie Monster green, Angie? He should be blue."

"These aren't the Cookie Monster," Angie said. "They're supposed to be Martians. Fat Martians. I couldn't find anything closer. Anyway, I'm also going to make some round, gray cookies that will be, of course, flying saucers."

"It sounds really hokey, Angie," Stan said, his speech a little garbled because some cookie dough stuck to his teeth.

"You think you could do better?" Angie snapped. His eye caught her rolling pin, and he backed away.

"You don't think anyone will be insulted by these cookies, do you, Derrick?" she asked.

"It's a charming idea, Angelina. The type that is very typical of you," he said with a dewy-eyed smile. Connie looked ready to throw up. "Of course, I think I've mentioned to you that aliens are gray, not green."

"How does anyone know?" Connie asked.

"Don't ask," Angie said as she finishing rolling out the last bit of dough. Stan took the bowl and used his finger to get out the last little crumbs. Angie faced Derrick. "Do you have any suggestions for what I should serve that would be in keeping with a UFO theme?"

He thought a moment. "No one has ever seen aliens eat. That's the problem. They're interested in cattle, but not as food."

"Interested in cattle? It sounds kinky." Stan laughed.

"Forget it Stan," Angie said, needing to move the conversation away from the subject.

She quickly finished baking the cookies so they could move on to brunch. Angie made omelets for Stan and Derrick, while she joined Connie with the Greek food.

Shortly after they all sat down to eat, she heard a loud knock on her door. She knew that sound. Homicide Inspector Paavo Smith had finally come to call. Her first reaction was joy, but then she looked at Derrick seated at her dining room table eating breakfast...

She pulled open the door, holding it in such a way that he could see into her living room, but not the dining area.

"Hi," Paavo said. She saw by his clothes that he wasn't officially on the job—jeans, blue tee-shirt, and black leather jacket, the collar upturned against the chilly fog—but she knew from experience he was most likely continuing to investigate on his own time. Still, just seeing him, her heartbeat jumped several notches. This would have been the perfect time for them to talk, if only she were alone.

"Hi," she whispered. "I'm so glad to see you."

"I had a couple questions after our talk last night," he said.

"Oh, okay." She had hoped he simply wanted to see her again.

"Something smells good," he said. When she didn't step aside for him to enter, his brow crossed. "Are you busy? Would you like me to leave?"

With a baleful glance over her shoulder at the motley crew, she stepped back from the door. "Of course not! Come in. Join the crowd. A few other people also dropped by this morning."

He walked into the apartment. Seeing him, Stan and Derrick both stiffened, and all three at the dining room table gave awkward little waves. Paavo glanced at Angie, but didn't say a word.

She tried to smile. "Derrick is staying with Stan for a few

days," she said, lightly resting her hand on Paavo's arm. "Want to join us? We've got plenty of Greek food. Connie brought it."

Paavo's gaze leaped from her to them. "Sure." His expression impassive, he strode into the dining room.

Angie's place setting was at one end of the table. Derrick sat at the other and Stan and Connie on each side. Paavo took an extra chair from the side of the buffet and placed it beside Connie. He took off his jacket and when he turned to place it on the arm of an easy chair, three pairs of eyes widened at the sight of the handgun at his back, tucked behind his waistband. He removed it and placed in his jacket pocket, then returned to the table and sat.

Connie greeted him warmly. Stan squawked a tiny hello. Derrick nodded. Angie dashed into the kitchen to grab a plate, napkin, fork, and glass for iced tea. She spread them before Paavo and he took a little moussaka and pilaf.

Conversation at the table ended as everyone gave their full attention to eating.

When he finished eating, Paavo said, "Holton, I hear you're staying with Bonnette."

"Yes," Derrick said, nodding, clearly uncomfortable with the harsh glare Paavo was giving him.

"Why is that?"

Derrick cleared his throat nervously. "Well...things are happening. Strange things. A disappearance, even a death—as you know. I'm a bit nervous, I guess."

"A death?" Stan whispered to Angie.

"Don't worry about it," she quickly whispered, keeping her eyes on Paavo.

"Have you heard from Mosshad yet?" Paavo asked Derrick.

Derrick looked at Angie for help, but she concentrated on her moussaka. "No. I tried calling. There's still no answer."

"Did you go to his house?"

"He lives in an apartment."

"Do you know his address?"

"Yes. I went there once."

"Since he's been missing?"

"No, but I phoned many times," Derrick said, not hiding his annoyance at the questions. "He never answered."

"Does he live alone?" Paavo asked.

"As far as I know."

Paavo wiped his lips with his napkin and placed it beside his dish. "We should check his place out, Holton."

"Oh, but..." Derrick turned to Angie again.

She shrugged.

Paavo returned the gun to his back and put on his jacket. "Thanks for the meal, Connie." He eyed Holton. "Are you ready?"

Derrick gulped down his coffee.

Paavo walked to the front door and opened it. "Let's go. We want to be sure the man isn't lying there unconscious, or worse, don't we?"

Angie stood, not leaving the table, but waiting for Paavo to make some sign, some gesture, that he still wanted to speak with her.

"Yes, I, er..." Derrick glanced woefully at Angie. "Glad you like the doughnuts, Angelina. I'll call you."

"Bye," she called.

Paavo lifted one eyebrow slightly as he glanced back at her, then followed Derrick out the door.

Angie stood frozen, looking at the shut door and not knowing what to think about what had just occurred. Why hadn't Derrick gone to check on Mosshad? What did Paavo want to ask her? To watch two men who had both been so close to her go off together was unsettling at best. She sank into her chair and scarcely noticed when Connie patted her on the shoulder.

Derrick sat scrunched against the passenger door of Paavo's Mustang.

"Which way?" Paavo asked, starting up the car.

"Head for Ocean Avenue."

They rode in silence. Derrick hugged his jacket tight against him. "It's freezing out. Cold for June."

"It's about sixty-five out there," Paavo said. "Typical summer in San Francisco."

"Yes, but it's a damp sixty-five. That makes it feel colder."

Paavo glanced at him and said nothing. The temperature inside the car seemed to drop even further.

"How much chance is there Mosshad has gone off on his own and is all right?" Paavo asked after a while.

"The guy is strange, but I doubt he'd do that."

"Who came up with the fake abduction idea?"

Derrick blew on his hands. "Can you turn on the heater?"

"It is on." Paavo waited for a reply.

"The abduction was just for fun," Derrick said. "It's the kind of thing that goes on in ufology."

"Hoaxes?"

"Stunts."

Paavo stopped asking questions as he zigzagged across Market Street. Between never-ending construction and the way the streets met at odd angles, it was always an adventure to negotiate.

Derrick cleared his throat. "Um, may I ask—aren't you investigating those bizarre murders where the bodies were mutilated?"

"Yes."

"There were three, right?" Derrick asked.

"Why?"

"Just curious about the numbers the newspapers said were

on the bodies. A seven, a five, and a four. Have you come up with what they mean?"

"No. Have you?"

"*Me?*" Derrick's voice screeched. "No. No, not at all. I'm a scientist. We play with numbers. That's all. They intrigue me. Any connection between the three men, by the way?"

"Nothing proven. Why?"

"No reason. Idle conversation. Forget I asked."

Paavo watched Derrick turn his head and stare out the passenger window while he nervously rubbed the fingers on one hand with those of the other. He found Derrick's interest in the mutilation murders significant, given all that was going on with the NAUTS, including John Oliver Harding's possible murder.

As they neared the Ingleside district, Paavo asked, "How close are you and Mosshad?"

"Not very. We both have an interest in space exploration, that's all. But, if you find Mosshad, or talk to any of the other people in our ufology group, I'd appreciate it if they don't know I'm staying at Stan's place. I'm creeped out by Oliver's death and the mutilation murders."

"Tell me about this guy who calls himself Algernon."

"There's not much I can say except he's a con man, living off donations gullible people give to the Prometheus Group, which he heads. He's no scientist. He knows nothing about real ufology."

"Do you know how to reach him?"

"No. Nor would I want to."

"Any reason to think he's dangerous?" Paavo asked.

Derrick scrunched his mouth. "Only if you're an attractive female."

Paavo grimaced at that. "Back to what you were saying about the murders, any reason in particular, other than Oliver

Harding having been a friend, that the murders have bothered you so much you want to stay with Bonnette?"

Derrick glanced at Paavo, then stared straight ahead at the moving traffic a long time before answering, and then it seemed as if all the questions he'd been wrestling with tumbled from him at once. "If Harding's death was an accident, why was he hanging out on the ledge of an upper floor window of an empty warehouse in the first place? If it was a suicide, what drove him to it? If, however, it wasn't a suicide or an accident, then who killed him? And why? And what about Mosshad? I thought he was just hiding to annoy us, but what if he's not hiding? What happened to him? It... it makes me believe one of us, someone who attends our meetings, or shares our interest, is behind all this."

Paavo nodded and continued on to Mosshad's apartment. When no one answered Mosshad's door, they contacted the apartment manager. Seeing the detective badge, she opened the door to them.

There was no sign of any disturbance in the small studio. Only signs—mail stacked-up, crusted food on dirty dishes—of an apartment that had been empty for a number of days. They thanked the landlady and left.

Paavo drove Derrick to the Hall of Justice and escorted him to Missing Persons to officially begin a police investigation of Mosshad's disappearance.

Paavo agreed with Derrick's idea that there could well be a connection between Oliver Harding, Mosshad, and the mutilation murders, although he couldn't see what it was yet. But it wasn't lost on him, either, that the objects left with the mutilated bodies were among those types supposedly reverse-engineered after an alien spaceship landed in Roswell.

He pressed the elevator button to the fourth floor, as Derrick's questions played in his mind. Seven, five, four. What could those numbers mean to Derrick? To a mathematician?

Seven times five times four? One hundred forty? Or add them, sixteen? What else?

Derrick's question about a connection between the victims caused his thoughts to travel along a new path. Because the three men had been so outwardly different, he and Yosh had been working on the assumption that the killings were random.

What if they weren't? What if there was some connection between them despite their surface differences? He sat at his desk. The day had begun as a day off, but he'd already shot that concept to hell. Why stop now?

He gave Angie a call.

"Paavo, hello." Her voice was soft, breathless, as if she was surprised and happy to hear from him. "Is everything all right? Did you find Dr. Mosshad?"

"Everything's okay. Mosshad wasn't in his apartment, so your friend is now filing a missing person's report on him," Paavo said, then quickly—so she would realize this was a business and not a personal call—added, "do you happen to know how I can reach Algernon? I remember he's your guest of honor."

"Oh... uh, yes. I don't have a phone number or anything else about him, but Connie and I visited an apartment where he was. I don't think it's his place, but somebody there should know how to reach him." She gave him the address, and before he got too nostalgic about hearing her voice, he ended the call.

Yosh, being a family man, was actually taking his day off, so Paavo went alone to the apartment Angie had told him about. It wasn't a great idea to go visiting a potential murder suspect alone, but he didn't want to waste a day.

It wouldn't have mattered. Algernon didn't live there and the woman who did said they communicated through the Prometheus Group's website to set up meetings.

She seemed so clueless; he believed her. He'd get computer

experts in the CSI staff to see if they could trace any of the messages there.

Talking to Angie about the UFO quacks suddenly caused him to remember seeing a brochure about Roswell in Bertram Lambert's trashcan. He hadn't even taken a photo of it; it had seemed so innocuous at the time.

He took out his notebook and flipped through it. Under Felix Rolfe, he noticed that some of the panhandlers around the ballpark had said Felix Rolfe spent a lot of time at Harvey's Liquors on Third Street. That was a potential lead he hadn't checked out yet.

He went to talk to the owner, an old man named Harvey. He remembered Felix Rolfe well, and spoke of how he'd run Rolfe out of his store at least once a week whenever Rolfe came by without money. The rest of the time, Rolfe could pay for the cheap whiskey he liked.

Harvey's red rheumy eyes went teary when he heard of Rolfe's death, although whether it was out of sadness at the loss of the man or the loss of a customer, Paavo couldn't tell. The old man directed Paavo to another friend of Rolfe's, Cheryl Martin, who lived down on Gilman Street in public housing with her three kids.

Paavo kept his hand ready to grab his gun as he walked down the littered, graffiti-covered halls to Martin's apartment, and did his best to look forward, backward and sideways as he passed doorway after doorway. This wasn't a place cops were welcome.

Cheryl Martin shed no tears when she learned of Rolfe's death, and readily told Paavo what little she did know: the street people Rolfe had known, liquor stores he'd visited, places he'd panhandled and anything else she could think of. He wrote it all down.

"Can you tell us when you last saw him?" Paavo asked.

"Las' week or so. I did' pay much attention."

"Did he talk about doing anything different from usual, seeing any new people, or anything at all new or special?"

She thought a moment, then smiled. "Come to think of it, he sure did. I didn' believe him, though. Glad I didn' or I jis woulda been disappointed. Now, I'm not. I 'spected something would happen when he tol' me, I jis didn' 'spect it'd be this bad."

"What did he tell you?"

"He said he'd joined some group with some fellas he met when he was in the Army. They had a drawing, and he won. He said he was goin' to collect him one hundred dollars, and after he got it, he was goin' to take me out to have a fine dinner. I knew better'en to believe 'im. Hell, if he'd a-won, he'd a-drunk it before I got that dinner anyways."

"Who was the group that had the drawing?"

"I don' know."

"Do you know where he was going to meet them?"

"No. He didn' tell me."

"Do you know anything at all about this group?"

"No. Oh, wait there's one thing." She began to rummage through a big stack of old newspapers and magazines and mail that covered the coffee table in front of the TV. "Here it is. He said they give him this paper."

Paavo took the brochure from her hand and stared at it.

"Roswell: The True Story."

19

The following afternoon, Angie rearranged the yellow lilies on the dining room table, and straightened the pillows on her sofa one more time, then paced back and forth. Her company was late. Maybe they had changed their minds? If so, she could end this fiasco of a Fantasy Dinner, which wasn't a dinner at all. It was too late for her to back out, but if Triana and Algernon didn't bother to show up...

But then she heard a knock on her door.

As Triana and Algernon entered her apartment, Algernon gazed deeply into her eyes and handed her a bottle of cabernet sauvignon from a vintner she'd never heard of.

"Thank you," she said, then took Triana's coat.

The two guests sat in the living room and Angie brought out a tray with prosciutto-wrapped melon balls, sliced kiwi, an assortment of petit fours, and strong Italian roast coffee from North Beach.

"The view from this apartment is incredible," Algernon said, turning toward the window with its view of the Golden Gate, Alcatraz, and the hills of Marin County beyond the Bay.

"Your things are way cool, too," Triana said, running her

hand over the arm of the sofa. "Are these real antiques or reproductions?"

Angie was taken aback by the question. "Real."

"I never could tell myself. Ooooh, yummy!" Triana reached for a petit four on the coffee table and plopped it into her mouth.

Algernon took a seat on the sofa, crossed his legs, and then picked up a piece of kiwi. Catching Angie's gaze, he curved his lips around the kiwi for a long moment before he pushed it into his mouth, then didn't let go of her eyes as he chewed. *What a slime,* Angie thought, then cleared her throat and concentrated on her coffee cup.

"Well," Triana said. "About your plans for the dinner. You've kept me in suspense long enough. Do tell us everything."

It was showtime. Angie drew in her breath. "I'd like to use the theme of Roswell."

Triana's lips turned downward at the name.

Angie hurried on. "Everyone seems to know the story, and it would be easy to build a fantasy about it. Women could dress up in 1940's outfits—high heels with ankle straps, tight slinky skirts, short fitted jackets with shoulder pads, their hair done up in poufs on top, then pulled back and smoothed to a roll or a cascade of curls at the nape of the neck—a very Joan Crawford or Betty Grable look. Men could wear old army uniforms, those starched and polished khaki ones, like Eisenhower or Patton. Or people could dress up like an alien if they wished."

Triana thought a moment. "It has possibilities." She turned to Algernon for his reaction. Busy eating a prosciutto-melon ball, he simply nodded.

"I like it!" Triana said immediately, with a big smile. "We can even work up an act, if we can find a third person to join us, and do a sort of Andrews Sisters routine, like that song about the boogie-woogie bugle boy of Company B."

"Sure, 'anything goes,' which might be another song from

back then," Angie said with a laugh, delighted at Triana's reaction to her idea. "Although Roswell happened after the war, not during."

"Whatever. That long ago is all ancient history to me," Triana said with a giggle.

"We can watch some old TV shows—Jack Benny, Milton Berle," Angie mused. "I guess they were from that period."

"Oh! Oh! I've got it, sweetie! 'War of the Worlds!'" Triana cried. At Angie's confused expression, she explained. "Orson Welles put on a radio show back then. It was about alien invaders. It caused a panic! People went flipping by on the radio dial—there was no TV or internet—and stopped at what sounded like real news to them. They heard little green men were invading us and flipped out! We could play it over loud speakers. What do you say, Algernon?"

He wiped his fingers on a napkin. "I believe your original concept is one of humor, to let people come to the event and be joyful," he said grandly.

"People usually go places in hopes of having a good time," Angie said, pointing out the obvious.

"But in this case, we need to be more serious," he explained. "This is not a good-time issue. While I agree with the theme of Roswell, we must handle it with dignity."

"I agree," Triana announced. "You're so smart, Algernon. And I really didn't care for that bugle boy song, Angie."

Angie's heart sank. "What about the costumes?"

"I don't think they would contribute to the seriousness of the affair," Algernon stated as if he were royalty giving a pronouncement to the "little people."

Why in the world did they hire me, then? Angie kept her voice even. "The whole idea of a Fantasy Dinner is to allow people to take part in the fantasy of the event. I think it would enhance the reality of Roswell if we allowed the attendees to come dressed for that period. They would know, and feel, what it meant to be in Roswell on that historic day over seventy-five years ago when the spaceship crashed. The event would seem far more real to the participants because they'll be living it."

"Hmm." Algernon put his hand to his chin and pondered this. "You may have a point."

"Also, I'd like to set up a pictorial display of Roswell from newspapers of the time. We'll use poster-size reproductions of them, plus old *Life* magazines, or whatever magazines they had. It would be a nice touch. And just think how interested the press will be in something like that."

"I like it. Some fun, plus seriousness, side by side," Algernon said. "I'll even have the Prometheans build a replica of a flying saucer."

"Yay! My thinking exactly!" Triana cried, girlishly clapping her hands.

"Afterward, we will become serious," he said. "I will talk to the people in attendance, to let them know about me and the Prometheus Group. We will need to give the press information that they can write up in their newspapers and magazines. After all, this whole event is for publicity."

"Of course," Triana cried. "We'll get you a world of publicity. I'm working very hard on it."

"I'll be sure to set up a fantasy exactly the way you want it," Angie added.

Algernon gave her a long, smoldering gaze. "That's what I hoped you'd say."

"What are you thinking?" Yosh asked Paavo as he stepped onto the Hall of Justice elevator and hit the button for the fourth floor. They had just finished talking to Ray Faldo about the early versions of a circuit chip and fiber-optic cable found on their last two victims. Faldo had learned such items were pretty much kept in storage by the military or in laboratories or museums. They generally weren't owned or borrowed for study by an individual.

"I'm not sure, yet," Paavo said. The elevator doors slid shut. "All the materials left with the victims have developed into equipment that has changed our way of life. Many people believe such items were reverse engineered after the crash at Roswell. We found a brochure about Roswell at our first victim's home, and the second victim's girl friend said he'd won a hundred dollars from a group connected with the Roswell brochure... Wait a minute," Paavo murmured, suddenly remembering—

"Of course!" Yosh said, with a smile. "Bertram Lambert's sister said he once won a pittance in a lottery—could that have been a hundred dollars? What if it was from the same guys?"

"That's right." Paavo thought a moment. "That could well be the connection?"

"I'd say so." Yosh nodded. "Plus, those UFO people talk about aliens abducting humans, doing mutilations, and being interested in our sexuality. It's sick, but it could be connected."

The elevator doors opened and he and Paavo got off on four where Homicide was located, but then Paavo put out his arm and stopped the elevator doors from closing. "There's one way we can nail down a connection between all three mutilation murders and the NAUTS with their lottery drawings and Roswell brochures. Shall we try it?"

Yosh grinned. "I got you. Let's go."

The two got back on the elevator and Yosh hit the button marked one.

"Sorry to bother you, Mrs. Cole," Paavo said gently as he stood in the doorway and spoke to the wife of the third mutilation victim, Leon Cole. She had been a lovely older woman two day earlier, but now she looked a good ten years older, her face lined with grief.

She invited him and Yosh into the living room to sit.

"I have a strange question to ask," Paavo said. "We are looking for any kind of links between the men murdered the way your husband was."

Her eyes rounded and she nodded.

"We were wondering if Captain Cole ever said anything to you about UFOs. Did he have any interest in them?"

"You're talking about those space things? Like all those science fiction movies coming out now trying to scare poor, God-fearing people?"

"Yes," Paavo said. "More or less."

She shut her eyes a moment. "Leon didn't care none about that trash. He was a good man. Even when he was stationed at Nellis Air Force Base in Nevada, he tried to stay clear of it, hard as it was for him."

"What do you mean?" Yosh asked.

"Nellis is near Area 51. That's where Dreamland is located, out at Groom Lake. It's a research center and secret air base. There's all kind of stories about the place—like they have dead aliens and lots of materials taken off of alien space ships that the government has reverse engineered. Lord only knows what all's out there, and I doubt He approves."

"Was your husband involved in any of that?" Paavo asked.

"Leon went out there a few times and got a little too close and too interested in all that nonsense to suit me. It's the work of the Devil as far as I'm concerned. Then something happened. He never said what it was, but right after a bomb went off in a lab, killing some scientist out there, Leon requested a transfer. He stopped having anything more to do with all that nonsense." But then she rubbed her forehead, and her confused gaze met Paavo's. "Until recently."

"What happened recently?" Paavo asked.

"There was a drawing. Some UFO group held it. Oh, my, but Leon was so excited! He won a hundred dollars because of Roswell, of all things. I told him I didn't want that money in my house!"

"So, Leon actually won the drawing?" Yosh asked.

"The day he disappeared, he was going to collect. I don't know if he got the money or not. I wonder if somebody killed him for that lousy hundred dollars!" She pulled out a handkerchief and quickly wiped her eyes.

"Do you know anything about the group, Mrs. Cole?"

"No, nothing. All I've seen is a brochure about 'Roswell, the true story', or something, that he brought home. It's on his bureau with a bunch of other stuff. I just haven't had the heart to clean it up yet. I'll go get it for you."

As she walked away, Paavo caught Yosh's eye. "Bingo!" Yosh said.

20

Angie was shocked when she heard the familiar knock on her door. It was only five-thirty; Paavo almost never left work when his shift ended. She'd been reading about the HAARP project in Alaska that government conspiracists said controlled the weather. There were times she wished the government were half as clever as the conspiracy theorists believed it was, and other times she was glad it wasn't. She put down the magazine article and ran to open the door. Cops had a way of knocking in a no-nonsense manner: open up or else. She figured they must teach it at the police academy.

"Paavo." She couldn't stop the big smile that filled her face and just seeing him again. "I'm sorry about Derrick and Stan and Connie here yesterday. If I'd known you were free and wanted to talk—"

"Don't be sorry. They're your friends." He walked with her into the living room. "I'm not crazy about a couple of them, but that's my problem, not yours."

"I can't believe you're already off work. Can you stay for dinner? I can easily put together something."

"Tempting as that is, Angie, I'm still working."

"Of course. I should've realized..." She sat on the sofa, her posture stiff, and watched as he removed his jacket and put it on a chair, then took off his shoulder holster.

He joined her on the sofa. "For some reason, your friend Derrick Holton was asking me about the numbers on the murder victim's chests—seven, five, four. Do they mean anything to you? Anything, possibly connected with what you've heard them talking about UFOs or little green men or anything?"

She shook her head. "Not a thing. Heaven only knows what Derrick's thinking. I'm worried about him, Paavo. He's on edge, or maybe over the edge."

"So I've noticed. One thing Yosh and I just learned, and we'll keep out of the newspapers, is that very likely there's a link between the mutilation death and Roswell and John Oliver Harding. Our victims all apparently attended at least one NAUTS meeting, and all three of them were winners of the $100 'jackpot' drawings being given out. Harding was the one giving out the sweepstake forms. He may have been the one meeting them to give them the money."

She couldn't stop a shutter. "Wait a minute." She rushed into the den and when she returned, handed him the same brochure as his victims had, *Roswell: The True Story*. "Will this help you any?"

He took the brochure. "Where did you get it?"

"From Harding, just as you said. He handed them out at the door to events. He seemed to be such a gentle, nice man, I can't believe he killed and mutilated people!" She sat beside him again. "I only spoke to him a couple of times, as I told Inspector Mayfield. In fact, the last conversation I had with him was about you."

"Me?" Paavo looked stunned to hear that.

She nodded. "He asked if I was seeing Derrick, and I said no, that I was seeing a homicide inspector. He said you should be with me, and I told him you were busy trying to find the mutilation murderer. He never read the papers or listened to the news, so it surprised him."

Paavo's eyes narrowed. "He didn't know of them?"

"So he said, but that's not the strangest part. When I mentioned Felix Rolfe, Oliver turned ghostly pale and then practically ran away from me. That was the night he died."

Paavo stroked his chin. "I wonder if he realized we were onto him, knowing that Rolfe was one of the sweepstakes winners."

Angie shook her head. "I don't know. When I asked him if he knew Rolfe, he said he didn't. He really sounded as if he was telling the truth, but he was also really upset."

"Did you tell Inspector Mayfield any of this?" he asked.

Angie's mouth tightened. "No. She cut me off so I never even got a chance to mention any of it to her. In fact, I'd forgotten about it until just now."

Paavo visibly shuddered as she talked about her exchange with Rebecca, and then he said, "This can't be coincidence, Angie."

And coincidences, Angie knew, were something Paavo didn't believe in.

"The people I've met at the NAUTS are strange," Angie emphasized, "but I hate to think any of them are killers."

"If we can find out why these murders are happening—the motive—then the killer will become evident."

"I just hope Derrick has nothing to do with it," she said softly.

"You still care about him, do you?" His voice was low but firm.

"Only as a friend. But Connie is seriously interested in him. And I was the one who got the two of them together. If I ever think about match-making again, Paavo, will you tell me to keep my nose out of it?"

He couldn't help but crack a smile as she said that. "Sure I will. And I'm sure you'll listen and do exactly as I suggest."

"Don't I always?" she asked.

"One last question," Paavo said. "The apartment where you met Algernon was a dead end. How are you contacting him for your Fantasy Dinner event?"

"Through the woman who's hosting it, Triana Criswell." She picked up her phone and send him Triana's contact information.

When it reached his phone, he stood. "Thanks. I should get going."

"Okay," she said, disappointed. But then a thought struck. "The NAUTS are having a meeting at eight tonight at Tardis Hall to talk about Oliver's death. And maybe some of them know how to contact Algernon. If you aren't busy…"

Paavo's brows lifted. "I'm not."

"Great! You relax and I'll put on dinner. I have some of the beer you like in the fridge, if you'd like to grab yourself a bottle."

With that she rushed into the kitchen and began pulling out ingredients to make a pasta carbonara. She had prosciutto in her freezer that would take little time to defrost. She didn't want to give him time to rush off the way he'd been doing lately.

Almost immediately after Angie and Paavo entered the hall, Paavo spotted Derrick Holton. Paavo excused himself from Angie and went off to talk to Derrick alone.

Hands on hips as she watched Paavo walk off, she decided to do some questioning of her own. Later, when she and Paavo compared notes, it would be interesting to see which one picked up the truly "inside" information.

Angie spotted Sir Galahad setting up his projector. After a few words of greeting and condolences about Oliver, she steered the conversation toward Algernon and was stunned when Galahad told her his ex-wife was an Algernon devotee.

Galahad scowled as he explained. "She doth believe she is the reincarnation of an Egyptian goddess of yore, and that the knave is her god."

"She's Isis? I met her once. She also said Algernon is a reincarnation of Osiris."

He yanked old film off the projector and put a new reel on. "It's all nonsense." Angie noticed that he dropped his phony accent as soon as he had anything emotional to say. "Algernon wouldn't tie himself down with some cheap-ass divorcee. He doesn't care how jealous she is, or how many fits she throws. Isis is a placeholder until he finds what he really wants—a rich broad who'll help him get to the top of his line. He was having a fling with Triana Crisswell until her old man found out she'd donated something like eighty thousand dollars to him."

"What!"

"It's true. For old-man Crisswell, it was chump change, but he put Triana on a tight leash after that. Made her life hell. Algernon's looking elsewhere now. Judging from your clothes, car, and jewelry, I wouldn't be surprised if he didn't show up at your place one of these days."

"He already has." Angie's mouth wrinkled with disgust.

"There's a lot of money in UFOs these days," Galahad said with a scowl. "Prime pickings for knaves like Algernon, methinks. It wouldn't bother me a bit if whoever killed those three blokes would finish the job and get rid of him."

"Who do you think is behind these murders?" Angie asked.

He got close to her and whispered in her ear. "The government."

Angie marched away. Was there no talking to these people without hitting right up against their government conspiracy theories? In the distance, she saw the only sane one in the group, wearing a white shirt, tie, and navy blue slacks. "Hi Elvis," she said when she reached him. "How are you doing? I'm so sorry about Oliver. He seemed to be a friend of yours."

"Not really. In fact, I didn't even like him," Elvis said. "Stuffing his brochures in people's faces. No wonder somebody killed him."

"We don't know that for sure. There's thought he committed suicide."

"So they say. It might have been a clever murderer."

"Who would want to murder Oliver?"

"Isn't it obvious?"

"Not to me."

He tossed his head back and announced, "Derrick Holton."

"Derrick?" Maybe Elvis was as crazy as the rest of them. "You can't mean that."

"But I do. Oliver was a spy for Algernon, and Derrick found out."

Oliver, a spy? Angie found it hard to believe. "Even if that were true, Derrick couldn't kill anyone. He's as gentle as they come."

"Not where the NAUTS is concerned. I'm telling you, Oliver would get the names of people interested in UFOs at NAUTS events by giving them brochures and telling them they might make a hundred dollars in a drawing. Then he'd pass the names to Algernon, who would get them to join the Prometheans."

"Derrick wouldn't kill for a reason like that!" Angie said, even as she realized she had more information for Paavo—to tell him that Oliver gave the names of the dead men to both the Prometheans and the NAUTS.

"Whatever," Elvis said. "Anyway, I've got to go sign up some new members now that Oliver's no longer around to do it."

She couldn't imagine there being any new members.

Frankly, she couldn't imagine why this group had any *current* members. They were all nuts, and she had to wonder about her own sanity not calling Triana and canceling her fantasy dinner right now. But she had never been one to renege on a promise.

She excused herself and walked around looking for Paavo. He and Derrick still hadn't returned from wherever they were having their private confab.

The strange older man she'd talked to a couple of times walked by. He seemed to know a lot about this group. "Malachi, hello!" Angie called as she rushed up to him. "I was just talking to Elvis and I'm really troubled."

The older man stopped and studied her. "Be cool, sister. You're looking real stressed out. Elvis is just a kid. You shouldn't let him get to you that way."

"I wouldn't, except that he implied Oliver had been a spy for Algernon, and that Derrick might have found out and, and killed him!"

Malachi shrugged, looking no more concerned than if he was flicking away a fly. "Frankly, if Derrick were to go after anyone, it would be Algernon."

Angie couldn't believe these people. As she stood temporarily speechless, Malachi wandered off and disappeared as quickly as he'd appeared. She shook her head. He was definitely strange, although he didn't refute Elvis' idea about Oliver being a spy for the other group.

Just then, Paavo and Derrick emerged from the same area. The doors opened, a signal that the NAUTS meeting would begin.

Derrick headed into the meeting while Paavo joined Angie. They quickly left the hall so she could fill him in on all she'd just learned.

She told him about it as he drove her back to her apartment. He listened intently and thanked her, but once at her front door, to her dismay, he said good night and left.

21

In Homicide the next morning, after filling in his partner on the latest he'd learned about Algernon, the Prometheus Group, and I.M. Neumann from both Angie and Derrick Holton, Paavo contacted Triana Crisswell. She was able to give him Algernon's phone number, but she had no address, and explained that Algernon wouldn't tell her which hotel he was staying at. He claimed he needed to keep his whereabouts top-secret because he had too many followers constantly trying to talk to him, and ask his advice. And he was also afraid of being abducted by aliens.

Of course, Paavo thought, why not?

Algernon didn't answer any of Paavo's calls. He attempted pulling a GPS location using the phone number, but Algernon had blocked GPS tracking on it.

"Who would have imagined these mutilation murders could be connected to UFOs and aliens," Paavo said to Yosh when they were both back at their desks.

"I hate to tell you, Paav," Yosh shook his head. "Don't say that out loud or the San Francisco PD will put you on stress leave."

"Still, I need someone with a science background to look at it into what these 'ufologists' are saying and doing. I think I'll ask a favor of Ray Faldo again."

"Faldo's a good guy, but what if he opens his mouth where he shouldn't? Make this sound like some whacked-out cult stuff and there's no way you'll convince a D.A. to take it to court."

"Take what to court?" Rebecca Mayfield asked as she put her handbag under her desk and her jacket on the back of her chair. "Have you two figured out who the mutilation murderer is?"

"You're just the person we need to talk to," Paavo said. "We have a lead that might give some motive. Even a suspect."

"That's great," she said. "How can I help?"

"Tell us how the John Oliver Harding case is coming."

She sat down at her desk. "Accidental death. All we can figure is he went out on the warehouse's top story window ledge to be alone, to think, whatever, and the cement was slick because of the rain and he slipped. We'll be filing the paperwork soon."

"Harding distributed brochures about Roswell and handled the hundred-dollar sweepstakes sign-ups. Do you know anything about that?"

Rebecca frowned. "Yes, but so what? He had so much stuff about Roswell it was almost spooky. The guy was buggy on the subject. He not only had thousands of brochures but also a card catalogue of names of prospective members of his group as well as those who signed up for the sweepstakes."

"Did he choose the winners?"

"It didn't look like it. And there was no indication who did choose them. The whole thing was probably illegal."

Paavo caught Yosh's gaze. "If we can figure out who chose the winners that might be the key."

"Key to what?" Rebecca asked, looking from one to the other. "I don't follow."

"We're on to something, but we need proof," Paavo told her. "Do you have a problem if Yosh and I go over to Oliver's home and take a look?"

"He had a small studio apartment. You're welcome to check it out."

"Any relatives around that we can talk to?" Yosh asked.

"Not that I've found. His mother died a few months back, and I couldn't find anyone else close to him. Like I said, I'm ready to file a report that his death was an accident. If you can find something to stop me from being wrong, be my guest."

As the two men stood to put their jackets on, Rebecca leaned back in her chair, her lips pursed. "If you guys come up with anything major from what looks like a simple accidental death, I'll never forgive you. Or myself."

Paavo's hunch only grew stronger as he went through John Oliver Harding's tiny apartment. The man was definitely three cans short of a six-pack.

Boxes of unopened Roswell brochures filled every corner. Harding also had a stack of completed forms for the one-hundred-dollar drawing. Among them, Paavo found the names Bertram Lambert, Felix Rolfe, and Leon Cole.

The one thing that was missing was any kind of evidence to link Harding with the deaths of the three men. The strong possibility existed, as well, that Harding was himself another victim. Could he have fallen to his death trying to get away from the murderer? If so, that could mean the murderer was one of the three men in the hall with Angie when she called him. Each of the three—ex-NASA Holton, grubby Galahad, and choirboy Elvis—was, at minimum, eccentric and obsessive. Murderers came in all shapes, sizes and disorders. Sometimes, they even seemed absurdly normal. Paavo wasn't about to discount any of them.

"Hey, look at this!" Yosh said, holding up a key from a kitchen drawer filled with junk. The key had a chain with a label on it, "Mom."

Paavo called Rebecca to ask if she had located Harding's mother's address. She had. "Why do you want it?" she asked, after reading out the San Mateo address.

"Just curious," Paavo said.

He and Yosh locked up Harding's apartment and drove down the peninsula south of the city. Even though they were crossing into another jurisdiction, since they were looking at the property of a man who had mysteriously died in their jurisdiction, they could do so. The address was located on a narrow road at the top of a hill in San Mateo, isolated and separate from the many subdivisions that dotted the area. The front lawn was overgrown and weed-infested, and the house looked as if it hadn't been cared for in some time. They knocked, announced themselves, then tried the key. The door unlocked.

The small four-room home sat on a surprisingly large lot. Dirty pots and dishes filled the sink. In the refrigerator, the milk had gone sour, and much of the food was moldy.

"Looks like your fridge, pal," Yosh said with a laugh.

Everyone's a critic.

Nothing in the house gave any hint of Harding's obsession with Roswell. Paavo opened the back door. In a far corner of the neglected property stood a shed. The two men trooped through weeds to the building.

Paavo opened the door, and right in front of them, blocking their entrance, was an enormous telescope on a stand with wheels. "Good God," Paavo muttered.

"I wonder if he was communicating with the mother planet," Yosh said with a chuckle as the two wheeled the telescope out of the doorway and stepped into the shed. A putrid smell immediately hit them.

It took a moment for their eyes to adjust from the bright sunlight outside to the dark gloom within. Even after they were able to see again, it took another moment for their brains to register what they were seeing. Lined up on a table were three glass jars with lids. Floating in each jar was a body part, a male body part.

"Christ!" Yosh cried. He couldn't stop himself from gagging, and bolted back outdoors.

Paavo forced himself to remain in the shed, although disgust at the sight before him filled every pore. "He was one sick bastard," Paavo muttered. "These must be trophies from the mutilation killings."

"I'd say we've got the proof we need of Harding's guilt," Yosh said, still standing outside the shed and looking in as he spoke.

"What's the awful smell in here?" Paavo asked, eying the rest of the space once the initial shock had worn off.

"Formaldehyde?"

"No. It's much worse. Something foul." Paavo walked toward the far wall where a tarp covered whatever was back there.

Yosh pulled out his gun and reentered the shed, clearly spooked by its grisly contents.

As Paavo neared the tarp, the stench grew stronger with each step.

Finally, he placed one hand on his own gun as he lifted the tarp. At first, all he could discern were a bunch of blankets. Then a black, nearly lifeless eye opened and looked straight at him.

Startled, he jumped back. But then caught himself. Taking a guess, he spoke the only name that made sense to him. "Dr. Mosshad?"

22

Now, one day before Angie's Fantasy Dinner—which had morphed into a Fantasy Hors D'oeuvres and Snack Buffet—she was at the farmers' market at the Ferry Building to check out foods to serve, especially ready-made foods. With her were Connie, Stan, and Derrick. Since the food served would be simple, she decided to do the so-called "catering" herself.

Triana Crisswell still insisted that three-hundred people would attend the event. Angie doubted that many would show up, but just in case, Earl, Butch, and Vinnie agreed to help her set up and oversee the buffet. She was pleasantly surprised when Stan and Derrick, who was still staying at Stan's apartment, said they'd help as well, despite the event being for Derrick's arch rival. Once Connie heard Derrick was going to help, she also volunteered, despite the fact that he never had phoned her. Still, as she told Angie, a girl could hope.

Angie quickly settled on a baked ham, southern fried chicken, potato salad, and macaroni salad as the cornerstones of the buffet. She was able to find people at the market who would cook and deliver the foods directly to Tardis Hall. She gladly wrote out checks to cover the costs.

Plus, big in the 1940s, were Jell-O molds. She'd have lots of Jell-O molds—green aliens, red Mars, yellow stars and blue spaceships. She could make them, and she was already working on cookies.

Then, armed with a notepad, she and her friends walked through the market to come up with interesting side dishes that wouldn't require much cooking. She would make a list, decide what she most wanted to deal with, and then on the morning of the buffet, she would buy the food fresh.

But, of course, as they walked around, the topic of the NAUTS versus the Prometheans came up.

"You mean all this fighting is over the Great Pyramid?" Connie asked.

"The Great Pyramid is just one part of it," Derrick said in answer to Connie's question. "The Prometheans have some wild theory that the pyramids were built by people who came here from the star, Sirius."

"They can't really think extraterrestrials built the pyramids," Connie said.

"Not that they built them, but that they guided the building of them."

"That's even crazier," Connie scoffed.

"The proof is based on people called the Dogon in West Africa," Derrick explained. "They have ancient sand paintings that show aliens from the star Sirius. The aliens told the Dogon that Sirius, the brightest star in our galaxy, is actually two stars. Not until the mid-nineteenth century, using a telescope, was it discovered that the Dogon tribe was correct! Sirius really is two stars, the main one and a small dwarf companion. It is impossible for them to have known that unless celestial visitors told them."

"Well, doggone!" Stan cried.

The others booed.

"Here we go, Angie." Connie, the practical one in the group, pointed to the fruit stands. "You need to serve pomegranate, mangos, and papaya."

"Add figs and grapes," Stan said.

"Over there are artichoke hearts," Derrick said. "Though why I should be helping you choose food for a party to give my competitor more publicity is a mystery to me."

"It's because you're such a good friend," Angie said, madly writing the suggestions into her notepad as they were called out. "Artichoke hearts are good. We'll have a garden salad section, but only with imaginative vegetables—no celery or carrots—and with them, a big selection of dressings."

"Ah, over there." Connie dashed ahead, shouting to Angie. "Braised fennel, avocado, yogurt with cucumber. This is great fun!"

Angie stopped, stared, then turned and faced Derrick and Stan. "Come close," she whispered, her voice tense. When they did, she said, "Don't look now, but I just saw the same, strange man I've seen a couple of other places lately. He's standing by the flower stands watching us."

"There are lots of people by the flowers," Stan said. "Is he the guy near the carnations or the sunflowers? Or near the gladiolas?"

"I don't know!" Angie cried. "And I don't want to turn around to see which flowers he's standing by, for Pete's sake! He's the creepy-looking man with the black suit and sunglasses with black frames. How many of them can there be?"

Derrick leaned closer to Angie, his back to the flowers. "Is his face white and pasty, his mouth tiny, completely expressionless and when he takes off his glasses his eyes are almost white?"

Angie looked at him as if he were crazy. "I've never seen him with his glasses off," she said slowly. "But the rest is true. How do you know this?"

"He's one of the 'Men In Black.'" Derrick said, his voice a

raspy whisper. "You must have missed our lecture about them. They're sent from *up there*, or the government—we aren't exactly sure which—to stop anyone who has had experience with extraterrestrials from going to the press about it."

"They must be from the government, then," Stan said, hands on his skinny hips. "Because they've done a piss-poor job. Stuff about UFOs is all over TV and radio."

"But with no proof," Derrick said. "They're watching you, Angie, for some reason. Be careful."

"Me? Why me?" she asked. But Derrick gave no answer.

"That's too creepy," Stan said. "The guy you've described is gone, anyway. Let's get back to the food."

"Hey, you guys!" Connie called as she returned to them. "What's the hold up? I was already down at the breads. They've got warm honeyed Indian fry bread, plus black rye, baguettes, sourdough, croissants—are they bread?—brioche, even something called Nutella-stuffed pretzels, which I've never heard of."

"They all sound delicious," Angie said.

"Don't forget to serve bruschetta," Stan said.

"Come over here," Derrick called. "There are more cheeses than you can shake a stick at."

Angie stared at the cheeses. Her list was already longer than she could handle. Paring it down wouldn't be easy, but was necessary.

"I think it's time to sample the desserts," Connie said. "I'll grab that table in the corner, and you guys can get one of everything. We don't want Angie to make the wrong choices, now do we?"

"I like the way that woman thinks," Stan said. "Are you sure you don't want to marry me, Connie?"

"I'm sure. I prefer a man who works and makes a living. Guess I'm funny that way."

"I'll get us all some coffee," Derrick said.

"Nonfat lattes for me and Connie," Angie said. "Stan likes

regular." She was already checking over the glass display cabinets filled with all kinds of pastries and other desserts—Charlotte Russe, pine nut-honey cakes, a variety of fruit tarts, chocolate blancmange, savarin Chantilly, puff pastry cakes with almond crème, a scrumptious marzipan-chocolate torte, and much more. It was serious salivating time.

Angie ordered a selection of the desserts—so much for Connie's plans to diet—and took them to the table where the others were sitting.

Derrick was talking. "I wish it were that easy. I've got to learn to deal with it."

"Deal with what?" Angie asked as she placed the tray of pastries on the table.

No one paid attention to her.

"What is it you're afraid of?" Connie gave Derrick a soulful look.

He rested his arms on the tabletop and hung his head. "It's so hard to talk about."

"What is?" Angie asked, as she carefully cut each pastry into four equal pieces.

"You can trust me," Connie said, lightly touching his wrist.

Derrick placed his hand on hers and smiled. Angie and Stan glanced at each other. Stan waggled his eyebrows. "It's because of them," Derrick said, gazing soulfully into Connie's eyes.

"Them?" she asked.

"*Them*," he answered, glancing upwards.

Uh, oh, Angie thought, *here we go again.* She handed out forks and napkins.

"I think they're here, Connie." Derrick gripped both her hands in his. "I think they walk among us, trying to learn about us. Trying to take us over. Make us part of their lives. Part of *them.*"

Just then a waitress came over with their coffee orders.

Connie never took her eyes from Derrick. "If you're talking about aliens, I don't believe in all that, and... and I don't think you should either, Derrick."

"It's not a matter of belief, Connie. It's a fact." His voice was firm.

Angie doled out some pastries, careful not to miss a word Derrick said.

"How do you know?" Connie asked, then took a bite of savarin.

He waited a long while, gazing into her eyes as she chewed, and when she didn't pull back, didn't look away, he lowered his voice and said, "Because, while I was working at Area 51, I was abducted for the first time. And they've come back several times since."

Stan, already on his third sampling of pastry, dropped his fork onto his dish with a clang. "Wow," he said, while Connie nearly choked on the savarin.

Angie froze. To think she'd been worried about Derrick saying something simple, like the end of the world was at hand.

"Impossible," Connie insisted as soon as her breath came back.

"I wouldn't lie about such a thing, Connie. Not to you or Angie." A longing gaze met Angie's before he turned back to Connie. In that moment, though, Angie knew he was telling the truth—*his* truth, perhaps, but he believed it. "It was the most devastating experience of my life," he continued. "I had no way to protect myself. I was completely at their mercy."

Connie's eyes, when they met Angie's, were troubled. "Where did this happen to you?" Connie asked.

"They come at night when I'm asleep. They come into my bedroom. Little men. Six of them. They're small, like boys, and they surround my bed, looking at me with those big, black eyes of theirs—frightening, cold, black eyes." He shut his eyes and drew in a deep, quivering breath. His face had gone pale and beads of perspiration appeared on his forehead. "Their faces are flat, with pointed chins. Some have said they have the face of a praying mantis, and they're right. It's what they're like. Like... like insects."

His voice turned low and shaky. Connie murmured words of comfort as she patted his arm. "You don't have to talk about it. Put it out of your mind."

He clutched her wrist. "But I see them in my mind.... They reach out for me. I try to run, but I can't outrun them. Their hands are like suction cups, taking hold of me. I'm afraid they want to do to me what's been done to three men in this city—horrible mutilations. But so far, I've been lucky. I don't know if I faint or what, because next thing I know, I open my eyes and I'm either in my car or on the ground beside it. It's crazy."

"You were drunk, man." Stan rolled his eyes. "I went to a party once and was slipped a molly and—"

"Be quiet, Stan!" Connie slid her chair closer to Derrick's and placed her hand on his shoulder. "You poor darling."

"So, did you see the inside of the spaceship?" Stan asked.

"If I saw it, I blocked it out. I don't remember," Derrick said meekly.

"I suggested he had nightmares and then sleepwalked," Angie said.

Both Connie and Stan frowned at her rational suggestion and turned back to Derrick, so she clamped her mouth shut.

"Jesus," Stan said with a shudder. "What a story."

"It's not a story!" Derrick faced him. "They're here. They came to me just last week. That's why I'm hiding. That's why I'm afraid to be alone."

Stan's eyes bugged out at this. "Wait! You're saying you're in my apartment hiding from ETs who want to cut you open?"

Derrick looked tearful. "I didn't want to tell you, afraid you wouldn't want me there."

"No shit!"

Derrick dropped his gaze to his clasped hands.

Connie touched them. "My God, Derrick, your hands are like ice."

"I don't feel well. It's the memories. I can't get rid of them. This last time, when they came after me again, it scared me so much." He shuddered.

"Let's get him home," Angie said standing.

"What am I supposed to do with him?" Stan shrieked. "I mean, if these creatures are real, and they know he's in my apartment..."

As Derrick stood, Connie put her arm around his waist and drew his arm over her shoulders. "It's okay, Stan," she said. "I've got my car. I'll take him to my house, give him some hot soup and let him relax. When he's himself again, we'll figure out if he can go back home, or somewhere he'll feel safe."

"Whew," Stan murmured, clearly relieved. "That's great, Connie. In fact, I'm sure I have a cousin who'll be visiting me. Starting, uh, tonight. Yes, I just remembered. Tonight. And he'll be staying a long, long time."

Derrick's hand gripped Connie's shoulder and his expression seemed to lose some of its pinched tightness. "You're a very kind woman."

She blushed and her eyes sparkled. "You're very brave facing all that."

Without a word to the others, they left the marketplace.

Stan and Angie sat down again, side by side and watched them go.

"Sheesh," Stan said, reaching for a marzipan torte. "I thought worrying about laser beams and radio waves was far out. That guy takes the cake."

"Cake I can deal with," Angie said, looking at the uneaten cakes and pastries in front of them. "It's Connie that I'm worried about."

23

"Congratulations!" Angie cried when Paavo opened the front door to his home that night.

She watched a smile cross his mouth, then brighten his eyes, even though they were dark-ringed and heavy with weariness. But then, almost as quickly, his smile vanished and he stepped aside so she could enter.

"What's this?" he asked as he took the plastic container she held.

"You and Yosh are heroes! It's all over the news. This is your reward for solving the mutilation murder case and saving Dr. Mosshad's life. I guessed that you might also be a hungry hero, so I brought over some home-cooking." She took off her coat and tossed it over a large easy chair. One sleeve flopped onto the seat and hit Paavo's cat, Hercules, on the head. Angie quickly petted him, begged forgiveness, and then marched into the kitchen.

Paavo's kitchen was large and old-fashioned with all-white appliances that were freestanding instead of built-in. It reminded her of the kitchen her grandmother used to have.

"I haven't turned on the TV or radio," Paavo said, setting the casserole onto the kitchen table. "What are they saying?"

"That Oliver Hardy, or Harding, was crazy. That after killing three men, he killed himself out of remorse."

She had brought a beef enchilada casserole—enough for three meals. She spooned a third of it onto a plate and covered it with plastic wrap. While Paavo put it in the microwave, she put the rest in the refrigerator, and noticed the risotto and chicken she'd brought him three nights earlier hadn't been touched. She tossed it in the garbage. *At least I tried*, she thought with a sigh.

"Did the press tell where he killed the men, or how, or explain the numbers on their chests?" he asked.

She faced him. "Did you give them answers to all that?"

"No. I'm still trying to figure it out. Not having facts hasn't stopped the media in the past, though."

"Did Mosshad have any explanation for Oliver kidnapping him?" She sat at the kitchen's wooden table. She liked sitting there, especially when the oven was on and the room warm and filled with the cooking smells of roasts or casseroles or pies. It reminded her of when she was a kid, sitting in her parents' kitchen in their old house, the one she grew up in before her father became rich. No matter how busy her mother had been helping her father with his growing business, she always had time for Angie in that kitchen.

The microwave dinged. Paavo grabbed a potholder. "Mosshad isn't able to talk yet. He was dehydrated and starving, and he's up in years. The doctors expect him to make it, but it'll take time. We'll ask him those questions when we're able, plus a few others. Like why did Oliver do any of this? Also, Oliver was short and heavy, but not muscular. How did he carry the bodies of those men? He had to have had help. Who helped him? And why on earth did he go out on that window ledge?

Did he do it to commit suicide? Did he simply fall? Nothing fits."

"Eat," Angie said. "Worry about it later."

The beatific look on Paavo's face when he removed the food from the microwave told her he was every bit as hungry as she knew he would be. As he grabbed a fork, napkin, and a bottle of Dos Equis beer, he said, "You really don't need to feed me, Angie, but thank you for this. It's great."

"I'm glad you like it."

He sat and ate, and she made herself coffee with the French roast she'd brought him. "You know, a really unfortunate part of these awful murders is that the UFO crowd is going to get a terrible black eye. The press will have a field day with these murders."

"That's a problem?" Paavo asked.

She paused and tried to put her feelings into words. It wasn't easy. "I've learned quite a bit from them about things in this world that are strange and interesting, and that I believe are really taking place. I'd say the UFO people aren't completely insane. For instance, when you think about space, the size of it, all the galaxies and how they go on and on, and then think about where they end, what's beyond the galaxies?

"The only part I'm not convinced of is that aliens have landed on earth. Of their existence, though, out there somewhere in the entire universe, whose magnitude is beyond human comprehension or understanding, why not? Who knows? And does the universe have an end point, a boundary? If so, what's beyond that? Not to mention, how did it all start? Many religions offer answers, but so far science cannot answer the most basic question of what caused the very first piece of energy or matter or light to form."

She guessed she'd gone too far, judging from the look on his face.

"As you mentioned, there are many things beyond our

understanding," Paavo said. "And, yes, I agree with all you just said. But my concerns tend to be much more worldly."

"So I've noticed, things like catching killers." She sighed. "Anyway, tomorrow night is my Fantasy Dinner at Tardis Hall. After that, I don't have to see any of the UFO people any longer. I swear, Triana Crisswell's fantasy has become my nightmare! I'm simply going to wing it, with the help of some friends."

"Connie?"

"Plus Earl, Butch, and Vinnie. Stan and Derrick offered, but I won't count on them." She opened the refrigerator to look for milk or half-and-half for the coffee and shuddered. Mustard, mayonnaise, and wilted lettuce were on the top shelf. A few other jars pushed far back and, she suspected, long forgotten. She drank her coffee black.

"Algernon will be attending, right? I haven't been able to locate him so far."

"He'd better," Angie said.

"Do you think you might have any success getting your friend Derrick and some other NAUTS there as well?" he asked thoughtfully.

Angie popped her head up from the refrigerator. Something about his tone when he said "your friend Derrick," hit her squarely in the pit of her stomach. "I'm sure Connie could get Derrick to join us with no problem, and where he goes, Galahad and Elvis often are. But why?"

"Your party might be the way to get some answers to the questions I still have about this case."

She shut the refrigerator door. "What do you mean? You found some remains of the dead men on Oliver's property. You found Mosshad there. What more could you possibly need? The case is solved, Paavo."

His gaze was hooded. "I wish I believed that."

His dinner finished, he put the plate in the sink and then he and Angie went into the living room.

"Coffee?" she asked.

"No. I'm going to try to get some sleep tonight, finally. It's been a busy couple of weeks."

She nodded. "You do look tired."

"About your Fantasy party, would you mind if I showed up at it? I'll even help, if you'd like. But I do want to finally meet Algernon."

"Of course. I'll be there at six, setting up. The party starts at seven."

He eased her toward the front door. "Okay. I'll see you then. And thanks again for the dinner."

"Great." There was nothing more for her to say or do. "See you then."

As she left his home, she thought this must be what being a good friend was all about.

24

"Angie, I'm so glad you're up already," Connie cried as soon as Angie pulled open the door to her apartment. "I was awake half the night. I couldn't sleep. I have to talk to you, and what I need to say, is best said face-to-face."

Connie's hair looked as if a cat had walked through it, she wore no makeup, and she had on a pink blouse with a bright yellow skirt. Angie immediately grew worried.

"Come in," Angie said leading her into the kitchen. "I didn't have the best night either. Can I get you some coffee?" she asked, wondering what could be so wrong.

"I'm not here for coffee," Connie said with a sigh.

Angie went ahead and poured her a cup just in case. "I'm making a Saint Honoré cake for my sister Maria. It's her mother-in-law's birthday, and this cake is her favorite, even though it's a bear to make."

"You're baking for your sister's mother-in-law when this evening you're putting out food for three hundred people?"

"I promised Maria a good month ago I'd make the cake for her, and you know Maria. I don't want to get on her bad side. Anyway, I doubt we'll get a hundred people, frankly, but I've got it covered. It's not going to be the hoity-toity affair Triana Crisswell expected by a long shot. I'm frankly surprised she's still putting it on. I only hope I get reimbursed for all the food she wants served."

Connie made no comment about Triana's dinner party as she dropped onto a chair in the kitchen. "We've got to talk. Seriously talk."

"All right. I'm listening." Angie picked up her pastry sack. She would fill sixteen miniature cream puffs with rum custard and then put them around the top edge of the cake. It was a beautiful sight. "But first let me say, I'm sorry about Derrick. You were great with him, although I realize, now, he's too strange. I should never have gotten you involved in any of this."

Connie placed her hands on Angie's worktable. Her face flushed slightly and a dreamy look filled her eyes. "Derrick is wonderful."

"He is?"

"Yes. That's why I'm here. As you know, he came home with me last night." She hesitated a moment, then the words gushed out, "Angie, I think I'm falling seriously in love."

Angie stared at her, her brain trying to make sense out of what she'd just heard. "With Derrick?"

"Of course, with Derrick!"

"But you've only known him a few days and the whole 'I-was-abducted-by-aliens' is kind of off-putting, don't you think?"

Connie blew off Angie's concerns. "Last night, at my house, I gave him split pea soup, then had him lie down on the sofa to relax. Before I knew it, I was lying down beside him. He stayed with me all night and we spent a lot of that time talking." She smiled and waggled her eyebrows. "And not *only* talking. He's so cerebral, so masterful, so sexy."

"Derrick?" The custard overflowed the little cream puff and oozed onto her hand and the counter.

"The thing that I'm concerned about is... Angie, does it bother you that I'm in love with your old boyfriend?"

Angie's eyebrows nearly reached the top of her forehead. She put down the pastry sack and began to clean up the mess.

"I know you wanted the two of us to meet," Connie continued. "I appreciate that. But women are strange that way. It happened to me once. I told a girlfriend about my ex-husband. She was unattached and interested, so I introduced them after warning her about all his faults. I never dreamed she'd see anything at all in the big dork. But she liked him! And the two of them dated for about six months."

"That sounds like a good thing," Angie said, wiping the tabletop with a sponge.

"It wasn't. I know it was my idea that they meet, but at the same time he was *my* ex-husband, and the thought of her with him, of her getting to know him in the same way as I had, well, I didn't like it one bit. It ruined our friendship. I don't want that to happen to us. You're important to me. I'll admit that I'd like to get to know Derrick a lot better, but I'm feeling guilty about it. So I came here to talk."

"I don't care if you date Derrick," Angie cried, tossing the sponge into the sink.

"That's easy to say, but think about it from deep, deep down, Angie. How would you feel in your gut about us seeing each other?"

Angie also sat down. Trying to decorate a cake while giving advice about love was impossible. "As long as you're not seeing Paavo, I don't care. That's from deep down, high up, wherever you want it."

Connie squealed and flung herself at Angie, nearly squeezing her to death. "You're a doll, Ang!" She perched on the edge of her chair. "Now you've got to help me. I just don't know where to start. What can I do to become a part of his life?"

Angie pressed her lips together as she wondered how honest she could be and not lose Connie's friendship. "Listen, are you really sure about this? Doesn't his belief in aliens worry you at all?"

"What if he's right?" Connie suggested.

Angie rubbed her ear to make sure her hearing hadn't gone haywire. "Right?"

"It's simple." At Angie's questioning look, Connie continued. "He followed his science until it couldn't answer all his questions. That was when he started looking for other ways to find answers and ended up with aliens. My ex was the same, but instead of aliens, he found drugs. I prefer aliens. Maybe we can help Derrick."

"I don't think so," Angie murmured.

"Angie, please! What if some *other* woman came along and straightened him out, and then she ended up with him? I need to try. I want to be the one to make him a normal, healthy, happy man, and then keep him all to myself."

"You care that much about him?"

"Absolutely. He's important to me. What can we do to help him?"

Suddenly, Paavo's idea that the NAUTS attend her Fantasy Dinner came to mind. "Well, from what I've seen," Angie mused, "Derrick would be a lot less stressed if the NAUTS and the Prometheans were friends again. Since Derrick offered to help me with the buffet at the Fantasy Dinner tomorrow night, maybe we should invite his close NAUTS friends as well. You and I could see that they and Algernon's people treat each other respectfully. By the end of the evening, they might be friends again."

"You may be right. If Derrick stops being so upset about the Prometheus Group, he might stop being so paranoid."

"Exactly."

"Angie, you're such a good friend," Connie cried. "Your idea may very well help me with my life!"

Angie just shrugged. "Sometimes, I surprise even me."

"You two are the luckiest SOBs alive!" Rebecca muttered as she walked into Homicide.

"Not luck, woman. It was skill, pure skill. Are we hot, or are we are hot!" Yosh bellowed. "I even brought home a bottle of champagne last night to celebrate." He glanced at Paavo and lowered his voice. "Turns out Nancy isn't nearly as crazy about her calligraphy teacher as I thought she was. She just likes calligraphy. Can you beat that?" He laughed.

"So that's why you're so jolly this morning," Paavo said.

"Yessirree. I still got it. Don Juan Yoshiwara, that's me."

Rebecca stopped at Paavo's desk. "Your celebration didn't seem to do you as much good as Yosh's. Or didn't you have one?"

Paavo frowned. "I'm glad we found Mosshad. And the evidence."

"You don't sound very glad," she said.

"Paavo thinks it was too easy," Yosh said. "Pointing to a killer who's dead sweeps a lot of questions under the rug."

"But the killer is dead," Rebecca said, as she sat down at her desk. "How much more justice can you get?"

"Maybe," Paavo said, more to himself than the others. Too much about this case still bothered him. When that happened, it was usually best to start again at the beginning.

Saying he'd be back soon, he left Homicide, got in his car and drove to Bertram Lambert's house. Since no one else lived there, it hadn't been turned over to Lambert's sister yet, and Paavo was still able to enter. In the bedroom he went through the box of photos Lambert had squirreled away in his closet.

The first time Paavo had flipped through them he hadn't been looking for anything in particular. He vaguely remembered one of them, however, and he wanted to check it out. It might have been nothing at all.

Paavo quickly found the one he'd been looking for. It showed an aged twenty-something Lambert squatting down on a dirt road next to three signs:

> WARNING
> Military Installation
> WARNING
> Restricted Area
> WARNING
> US Air Force Installation

He turned over the picture and saw a small notation: Groom Lake, NV. 2010.

Groom Lake was the location of Area 51 on the Nevada Test Site. The town of Rachel, where John Oliver Harding had lived, was the closest civilian town. The third victim, Leon Cole, had been stationed at nearby Nellis, AFB. Felix Rolfe's social worker had said that Rolfe had once been in the Army and had traveled throughout the Southwest. And now he had proof that Bertram Lambert had been there as well.

Area 51, Dreamland, where UFOs were said to have been brought and studied had to be the connection between the victims. It seemed farfetched, yet Derrick Holton had asked about the numbers on the victims' chests. Seven-five-four. Those numbers must have something to do with UFOs. Now, if only he could figure out what.

Derrick had clammed up when asked, but there might be a lot more talkative group at Angie's Fantasy Dinner. And Algernon would be there. Finally, the missing man in this investigation would no longer be able to hide.

Back at the Hall of Justice, Paavo gathered up all the information he'd amassed, printed it all out, and called Crime Scene Inspector, Ray Faldo. They needed to talk.

"Paavo, you need to listen to your partner about this. Yosh is right," Ray Faldo said that same morning. He and Paavo sat at a high work table in the crime laboratory. The criminologist took the papers Paavo had printed about supposedly re-engineered materials from the Roswell landing and fastened them together with a butterfly clip. "The investigation is over. Case closed. Take these materials and burn them."

"But they explain the implements found on the victims," Paavo argued. "Roswell, aliens abductions, crop circles, cattle mutilations, on and on. We have no motive for John Oliver Harding to be killing people and leaving those things behind. It makes no sense!"

Faldo handed the documents back to him. "The killer, Oliver Hardy or Harding is dead. Forget it."

Paavo took the papers, but wasn't ready to drop the subject. "The part that bothers me, Ray, is that John Oliver Harding had no scientific training. He enjoyed astronomy, but as an amateur. There's nothing that makes him sound like a psychopathic killer. And that makes me wonder if we've got the right man."

Faldo got up off the high stool he'd been sitting on and rubbed his back. He was perpetually round-shouldered, even when standing. Paavo guessed it was from spending too many hours hunched over a microscope in the lab. "Let me be clear, Paavo. You can't expect the higher ups to toss out the case against Harding as the mutilation murderer because he wasn't enough of a scientist. City Hall wants these cases off the front page!"

Paavo shook his head in dismay, while recognizing the truth

of Faldo's statement. "I can't help but think whoever killed those men did it because they all had some connection, however slight, to Area 51. That's why the killer used pieces of that early technology to prove he knows what he's talking about. Put it together and it simply doesn't sound like John Oliver Harding."

Faldo thought a moment. "In that case, you need to figure out where the killer got those early prototypes left with the body, because if Harding didn't leave them with the body, who did?"

That was exactly what Paavo wanted to know.

25

News and publicity could make or break an event. Just as quickly as news of Frederick Mosshad's abduction had caused a flurry of excitement and interest in the UFO community, and a concomitant surge in interest in Triana's party for Algernon, so, the opposite could and did occur.

When the story hit that the three men so horribly killed and mutilated were the victims of a follower of a UFO group, people in the city recoiled, and an outcry rose up from the public about the strange cults springing up in the city by the bay.

Angie didn't let the news deter her. She and her friends would present the Fantasy Dinner, as requested, for one-hundred-fifty guests—she had dismissed Trina's "three-hundred" number as wishful thinking—more of a fantasy, in fact, than the dinner would be.

With a sigh of relief, she realized her new business venture would be over in just a few hours. No one, other than Triana, had ever contacted her about holding a Fantasy Dinner.

Fantasydinnersare.us had become fantasydinnersare.finished.

And frankly, she didn't even mind that it hadn't worked out. The reality wasn't nearly the big hit she had imagined such a business might be.

Angie arrived early at Tardis Hall to put up posters and do whatever she could to set things up. The food she had ordered was delivered to the hall's back stage area on time. It looked and smelled delicious. Angie would arrange it on platters and chafing dishes that had an elegant flare, putting out a little at a time, as needed.

To her delight, Paavo soon arrived at the Hall. She was thrilled that he actually took off work early to help her... and to finally meet Algernon.

She ran up to him at the door.

"Look at you," he said. "I didn't know this was a costume event."

"Only for those who want to dress up." She slowly turned so he could get the effect of her pinched-waist maroon suit with huge shoulder pads, a wide collar, and white trim. The skirt was pencil thin and fell to mid-calf with a kick-pleat in the back. Her white, open-toed shoes were tall with chunky heels, platform soles, and ankle straps. She even found nylons with a seam down the back.

She patted her hat as she turned to make sure it was still on straight. It was maroon in color and pointed, with a long white feather angled across the back of it, and held in place with an old-fashioned, long hatpin. She felt like the reincarnation of Carole Lombard or Myrna Loy from an old classic romantic comedy. Or she had until she saw the look on Paavo's face.

"What is that on your head?" he had asked.

She explained that she had found the outfit in a 1940s magazine on the Internet, and her mother's dressmaker had worked round the clock to sew it for her. "Isn't it cute?"

"Words can't describe what it is," he had muttered.

"Hmm, thanks, I guess. Anyway, come see the area where the buffet will be held."

Round tables and chairs had been set up. A sound system was in one corner, and at one end of the room was a papier mâché flying saucer.

A sign over the back of it read Roswell, July 5, 1947. Paavo stared at it a long moment.

"Algernon's group built the flying saucer," Angie said. "Isn't it cute? And they put up the posters I had made from photos of the Roswell crash site and newspaper headlines. That's a photo of Jesse Marcel, who you told me was the first military officer who investigated the debris at the Roswell site and declared it was not from this world, and over there is Roy Danzer, the workman on the military base who claimed to have seen a live 'alien creature' along with several dead ones being carried into the military base, and whose life was threatened if he said anything. I simply love the way everything looks!"

"It's all great," he said. "Quite realistic...if such a thing can be realistic."

"I think it can," Angie said firmly. "And we're going to have a wonderful party, no matter how hard the *Chronicle* has tried to ruin the event, with bad publicity." She looked around the still empty room. "Well, no one else is here yet to help me, so would you help me carry the food from my car?"

"Sure." He followed her out to the parking lot where she had storage containers for both hot and cold food. He took the heaviest ones, and Angie took what she could carry.

"It's hardly the newspapers fault that they reported the story about Harding, Mosshad and the murders," Paavo said. "If you think that, you might say it's my fault for having solved the case... or hopefully solving it."

"You're right. I'm grateful it's solved, no matter how adversely it might affect the party." She sighed as she looked over the still empty hall.

Just then, Connie walked in. Angie oohed and aahed over Connie's vintage dress shop find—a blue polka dot dress with padded shoulders, short sleeves, a narrow belted waist and a full skirt. With it, she wore red shoes with chunky heels and had styled her blond hair so that the bangs were curly and the rest pulled sleekly back into a polka-dot bow so large and stiff it stood out from the sides of her head like wings.

Right behind her were Earl, Vinnie and Butch. They wore white shirts, white slacks, and white sailor's caps—they said that was military enough for them. Angie was afraid the three older men had all spent more time wearing jailhouse blue than military uniforms, but she decided not to bring that up.

Soon everything was in place, and they simply had to wait for the guests to arrive. Seven o'clock—the start time—came and went. People should have been arriving, Angie thought. But maybe ufologists were always fashionably late.

Not even Triana Crisswell or Algernon were there.

Derrick, too, hadn't arrived, and Connie didn't know where he was. So much for Angie's big NAUTS/Promethean reconciliation plan.

She also noticed Paavo didn't look happy about the missing Algernon. Where, she wondered, was her guest of honor, let alone Triana Crisswell, who was supposed to give her a check that night to cover the food cost, as well as her fee?

Ten minutes later, only ten people had shown up. They went straight to the buffet, eating as if they were on the verge of starvation.

Angie noticed Paavo take out his notebook and write something down. She went over to him. "What are you doing?" she asked brightly.

"Look." He turned his notebook so she could see it. "Roswell—7/5/47."

"Why did you write the date of the crash?"

"The men who were killed, on their chests were those same

numbers—seven, five, four. I think the killer was carving the date of the Roswell crash—July 5, 1947." His eyes narrowed. "I suspect your friend, Derrick, knew it all along."

Angie's shoulders sagged. Was this another deception from Derrick? "I admit it makes sense, when you consider how fascinated with Roswell they all are."

"All of them are interested in Roswell and there's also some connection with Area 51," Paavo said.

Angie remembered Derrick talking about the place. "Area 51 is where the Prometheus founder, I.M. Neumann, lived and died."

"Right," Paavo said. "It's not back to the future, but back to the past. That's got to be the key to what's really going on here."

Angie's mouth went dry as she said aloud what she knew Paavo had to be thinking. "There's still one number missing. The last seven."

His lips were firm. "I know."

Just then Vinnie put on a CD of "Pennies From Heaven." Connie grabbed Butch and dragged him out to the dance floor with her. He held her as if she were made out of glass, and smiled from ear to ear as he led her in a World War II-style jaunty two-step around the hall.

Angie laughed as they danced by, waving and grinning for all they were worth. Maybe this wouldn't be the big, classy party she had initially imagined it would be, but if people bothered to show up, she hoped they would have a good time. She checked her watch. Where were Triana and Algernon? They should have been here by now.

Vinnie kept the music going, but Connie soon bailed on Butch to catch her breath and then to go outside to wait for Derrick. As Angie's nerves about this disastrous event grew more frayed by the minute, a man in black, the same one Angie had noticed watching her from time to time, entered the hall and stood in a corner. "Oh, dear," she murmured.

Paavo's gaze followed hers. "Do you know him? He looks like something out of a science-fiction film."

"Let's check him out," she murmured. With Paavo at her side, she went over to the strange fellow. "Welcome. Are you a friend of Algernon's," she asked.

"No. Just a visitor." He turned his back to her, walked to a far corner and stood with his arms folded, looking over the small group of participants.

Angie glanced at Paavo. He took her arm, and they returned to the buffet. "That was strange," he said. "Looks like it's time for me to put on my shoulder holster and jacket."

She peered back at the man. "I suspect he's harmless. I've seen him attend a NAUTS event or two in the past."

Just then, Elvis and Sir Galahad walked in. "Hi, Angie," they said. They stiffened when they saw Paavo. They remembered him from the night Oliver Hardy died.

"Thanks for coming." Angie shook hands with them. "You're a little early, I guess. Just a few hungry people and the man in bla... Where did he go?"

"Oh? We were afraid we were late," Elvis said. "Where is everybody?"

"Also late," Angie said.

"Where's Derrick?" Galahad asked.

"He's not here yet, either. Connie's waiting for him out front."

"She is? I didn't see her," Elvis said. Galahad shook his head. "Me, neither."

"That's strange." Angie looked around. "Oh, I know. She and Derrick must have taken the side hall, around the auditorium, and gone straight to the backstage area. Connie probably thought I was already back there setting out the ham and chicken, which I probably should be doing, as a matter of fact."

"I'll help," Paavo said.

"Me, too, Miss Angie," Butch said, following her.

The backstage area was deserted. "How odd. I wonder where Connie and Derrick went?" Angie said. She dealt with quite enough disappearances in this strange place. "Well, let's get started. Everyone will be here soon, I'm sure." She took off her hat and put it on a high shelf so the feather didn't get broken.

Butch wandered off. "I'll look around for them."

"Don't go too far, Butch!" She glanced at Paavo. "I'll put some of this chicken in the metal pan that goes over the burners out on the buffet table. Do you know how to light the burners?"

"I think I can manage," he said dryly, as she filled the pan.

"There's something strange over here, Miss Angie," Butch called. Angie looked up and saw that he was near the stairs.

"Don't worry about it, Butch," she replied, then turned back to Paavo and the task at hand. She squeezed two additional pieces of chicken in the pan. "Here you go. If you would set it on the chafing dish, so it'll stay warm, I'll take care of the ham."

"Aye, aye, Cap'n." Paavo lifted the heavy pan and carried it into the auditorium.

"Miss Angie," Butch called. "I really think you gotta come see this."

She didn't have time to go see anything, but Butch wasn't one to bother about unimportant details, and it wasn't as if a hall full of people were clamoring for food. She put down the serving fork she'd been using. "See what?" she asked, walking toward him, following his voice. To her surprise, he was now standing at the bottom of the stairs in the warehouse basement. "What are you doing down there?"

"I noticed Miss Connie's hairpins. You'll see one of them at the top of the stairs and another on the stairs."

"Connie's hairpins? Whatever are you talking about?" She looked at her feet. Sure enough, a bobby pin was on the ground. She walked down the steps, searching each as she went. She saw another bobby pin on the middle step, another on the last one.

"When we was dancin' I noticed one was ready to fall off," Butch said. "An' Miss Connie tol' me she put a bunch in her pocket so she'd be able to keep her short hair pinned back with that big bow she was wearin'."

"So, she must have come down here for some reason," Angie said. She wondered why the door to the basement was open and why the lights were on. The night they had searched for Oliver Hardy, it had been locked. The basement floor was much like upper floors in the warehouse—nothing but rows and rows of large industrial shelving. "I wonder what Connie's doing down here?" she said quietly.

"I don' know, but there's another hairpin down that aisle."

They walked past it, and at the next four-way intersection of aisles between shelves, Butch spotted another hairpin deep inside one of them. "I don't like this," Angie said. She called out, "Connie! Connie, are you down here?"

They waited a moment, and when there was no answer, turned down the aisle with the bobby pin and continued to the next intersection of aisles. "Connie! Are you all right?" Angie called, louder this time. "Connie! Answer me!"

Butch kept going, looking for more bobby pins. He spotted another one. They turned again. "Wait," Angie caught his arm, stopping him. "We need Paavo. Something's wrong here."

"Maybe she's just havin' a little whoop-de-do with her boyfriend," Butch suggested.

Whoop-de-do? "But why leave the bobby pins?" she asked.

"To find their way back?" Butch suggested.

Angie thought about it. "It's not that difficult! Also, it's not like Connie to disappear when I need her. Look, I can't move fast in these heels or with this tight skirt. Will you run up and get Paavo? I'll wait right here."

"Sure thing. I'll be right back. Don' you move a muscle."

"Don't worry, I won't."

As she watched Butch head down the hallway, she almost regretted not going with him. This basement was creepy. "Connie," she called again. But her voice was decidedly smaller this time.

She walked just a little way forward, to the next intersection of aisles, and called again. Up ahead, on the ground, she saw something that made her heart stop.

She ran toward it and picked it up. Connie's hair bow. The worry she'd felt following Connie's bobby pins just increased a hundredfold. What, she wondered, was going on here?

26

Paavo was fiddling with the burners under the chafing dish when Butch rushed up to him and tapped him on the shoulder. "This contraption doesn't make any sense," Paavo complained. "I can't get the burners to turn on."

"I know, but, uh, you see, she went down to the basement," Butch said nervously.

"What's she doin' down dere?" Earl asked, his eyes round. "Ain't dat da place somebody got abducted from?"

"Shut up!" Vinnie ordered. "You're makin' me nervous. Watch the food, some a these turkeys think they should eat it all themselves and don't leave none for nobody else. You gotta set'em straight!"

Paavo kept turning knobs, trying to get the burners to light. "Why is she in the basement?"

"She's looking for Connie and needs help."

Paavo immediately straightened. "She needs help?"

"Yeah."

"*Why didn't you say that?!*" Paavo quickly turned the knobs to Off. "Show me where you left her."

Elvis and Galahad followed Paavo and Butch into the backstage area, leaving Vinnie and Earl to keep an eye on the buffet.

"We were following Miss Connie's hairpins," Butch said, going down the stairs to the basement.

"Like that one?" Paavo asked, spotting a hairpin on the ground.

"Yeah. Me an' Miss Angie followed them. But we don' know why Connie went down there."

At Butch's words, a chill rippled along Paavo's spine as childhood tales of Hansel and Gretel came to mind. But he was letting the creepiness of this place get to him, and pushed the thought aside. His voice turned cold and hard as he said, "Let's find Angie and get her out of here, then figure out where Connie's gone."

"The basement is like a catacomb," Galahad said, coming up behind them. "The door to the basement is usually kept locked. I guess the owner came by to make sure the place is empty since the building will be demolished soon, and forgot to lock up again."

"Who is the owner?" Paavo asked.

"I don't know."

Butch pointed to a bobby pin farther down a hall. Paavo was halfway to it when the lights flickered and then went out.

"Oh, Lord," Angie murmured when the area around her turned pitch black. *Come back on!* she prayed. But the lights didn't. And of course, her cell phone with its nifty flashlight was in her handbag up on the main floor with the food she should be serving.

The basement was darker than night. There were no windows, no light of any kind. She reached out her hands and walked slowly forward, searching for a wall to hug. It was bad enough being down there in the dark. Being in the dark without anything nearby to hold on to was intolerable. "Connie?" her voice was barely a whisper.

But then the thought struck her that, if Connie had been brought down here against her will, letting it be known that she was also here alone, wasn't such a great idea. The wrong person might find her. Butch should have Paavo looking for her by now. She should head back toward him.

She turned what she thought was one hundred eighty degrees, took two steps and bumped into a shelving unit. Which way *was* back?

She pressed herself against the shelves, afraid to move another step. But then, in the distance, she saw a ray of light. Unsure what the light was, she inched toward it. A door stood open and the room beyond the door had its lights on. Why did that room have lights when the area Angie was in, didn't? As she watched, a small person—man? woman? she couldn't tell—stepped out of the room and then shut the door. All went dark again, but she heard the person's footsteps—bold, running steps—heading away from her.

How could anyone run in this darkness? How could that person see in the dark?

She was about to call out, call for help, until some fear of who—or what—that person was, stopped her.

As the sound of the footsteps lessened, she realized there must be another way out of this scary basement.

She wasn't sure what to do. She felt trapped and frightened, all the while hoping the lights would come on, hoping Paavo could find her...

Her pulse raced and the growing silence caused all the eerie stories she'd heard recently about alien encounters rushed back at her.

"Angie!" Paavo called. He hesitated to call too loudly, suddenly worried that something much worse than Angie wandering around down here alone was going on. He turned on his cell phone's flashlight. "Angie, can you hear me?" His voice was a little above a whisper.

No answer.

The basement was filled with industrial free-standing banks of shelving in the middle of the space, making it a warren of aisles. He didn't like this at all.

"How far away is she?" he asked Butch.

"I ... I'm not sure. We just followed the hairpins."

One of Connie's "blonde" pins glittered in the flashlights beam just a few feet ahead of them.

"There's a good chance those lights didn't go out by accident," Paavo said. "Butch, you stay here and if anything goes wrong, run like hell for help. Elvis and Galahad, these thick cement walls are blocking cell service. You two go upstairs and call the police, give them my name and tell them to send reinforcements—something strange is going on here. And then try to find the circuit breakers and see if you can get these lights working."

Swearing at himself for not wearing his gun, Paavo moved forward, trying to find bobby pins to tell him which way Angie might have gone.

As soon as the lights in Tardis Hall went out, the few customers in attendance grabbed as much food as they could carry and ran from the hall.

"'Ey!" Earl called. "Stop t'ieves!"

The open doors brought moon and starlight into the Hall, helping Earl and Vinnie see a bit. They ran to the office.

"I foun' a phone," Earl said as he picked up a phone on the desk.

"The number is 9-1-1," Vinnie said.

Just then, the last of the customers left the Hall, and the doors slammed shut, plunging them in complete darkness once again.

"What's wit' you?" Earl cried. "You t'ink I ain't never called emoigency before? But maybe we should oughta jus' call PG&E."

"Call 9-1-1. Let the cops come see what's goin' on here. I don' like it."

"Uh, oh." Earl clicked the button on the phone a few times. "I don't hear no dial tone. I tol' you we outta get one a dose smart phones. Den we could help!"

"Quiet! I just heard a noise."

Footsteps grew louder, one by one, coming closer to them.

Vinnie and Earl stood by the desk as if frozen in place. The footsteps slowly approached the office, step-by-step.

"Shut the office door!" Vinnie ordered.

"Okay. If I can find it," Earl muttered. He moved slowly, Vinnie right behind him, but before they reached the door, the footsteps sounded very, very close on the linoleum floor.

The two men crouched down as whoever walked into the office stopped right next to them.

Although they didn't move, the intruder did. He took a step tripped when his leg bumped into Vinnie, crouching low on the ground. He cried out as he fell forward and landed on top of Vinnie.

"I caught him!" Vinnie shouted.

"I got him, too!" Earl said, wrapping his arms around the guy's legs.

"Kick him! Gouge his eyes! Hit him in the nuts!" Vinnie yelled.

"Stop! It's me—Elvis," their captive cried. "Paavo said we've got to call the cops, quick! But the hall's wi-fi is out, and cell reception isn't good here, so I'm trying to find the office landline."

"I t'ink," Earl said as he let go of Elvis and stood up, "we got some bad news for you."

27

Angie tried to ignore the scary thoughts of aliens and UFOs parading through her head. Instead, she tried to think of more earthly things, like why there was light in the room that the strange figure had been in, but nowhere else in the basement? Was there something special about that room, or instead of a power outage, had someone purposefully shut off only the main basement lights?

The bobby pin trail might have been heading toward the lighted room. Could that be where Connie was? Had Connie been forced into that room? Angie's instincts told her yes. Why else would Connie have left a "bobby pin" trail?

But who would do such a thing to Connie?

Holding her hand against the shelving, Angie made her way along the basement, going in the direction of the room where she hoped to find Connie. When she reached a solid wall, she continued along it until she came to the frame of a door—very likely the door she'd seen the strange figure emerge from. She found the door knob, and holding her breath, turned it.

The latch clicked.

Pushing the door open, the first thing that hit her was the smell—metallic and acrid. The room was lit in the garish fluorescent lighting of a hospital and she had to blink a couple of times to help her eyes adjust to the sudden brightness. It was a laboratory with shelves and counters lined with bottles of chemicals, beakers, a Bunsen burner, microscopes, flasks, condensers, and a whole litany of other laboratory implements.

She opened the door a little farther, and there, kneeling on the floor, her hands and ankles bound, her mouth taped, was Connie.

"Connie," she whispered as relief and fright filling her.

Stepping into the lab, her gaze swept over the room.

What she saw on the far side caused her to gasp, not wanting to look, but needing to.

Paavo stood in the darkness, his frustration higher than he'd ever felt it. All he could do was to keep moving forward, his every thought was about Angie.

His instincts told him there was something seriously dangerous happening here. It wasn't just a coincidence that the lights happen to go out as Angie and the others were following Connie's bobby-pin trail. His nerves crackled with fear for both women. But his mind was all about Angie.

What if she had been captured? What if something happened to her, what if something was happening to her right now? Images of the shockingly mutilated bodies filled his head, and he was convinced whoever did that to those men was behind the strange circumstances going on in this Hall. The thought of anything like that happening to the woman he was in love with, despite all his foolish refusals to accept that fact, angered and horrified him.

He should have been with her. He should have listened to

her. While he was trying to convince himself that matters of the heart could be relegated to logic and rationality, all he was doing was making matters worse for both of them.

He needed to put his analytical mind to use now, to help him find the only woman he ever deeply cared about, and get her away from this madness. All he could do is pray he wasn't too late.

His practical nature forced him to look at the whole picture. Connie was interested in Derrick, which meant she was probably with him. Derrick had been paranoid that someone was after him, and potentially, it wasn't just paranoia—he might have been right.

Everyone, both the NAUTS and Prometheans, knew Derrick would be here this evening. If Derrick was the target, and Connie was with him, she might have gotten involved due to bad luck and bad timing. Once Derrick was caught, then Connie was as well—but she'd been smart enough to leave a trail for someone to find them.

Of course, Paavo could be completely wrong, and Derrick had snapped, captured Connie and dragged her along with him...

But Angie trusted Derrick, despite everything.

He wasn't sure what to think, except that Angie and Connie were here somewhere and their situation could be desperate.

Who was behind this, though? Which of the NAUTS or Prometheans could it be? Algernon? He still hadn't shown up, but from everything Paavo had been able to find out about the guy, including the way he managed to conceal his whereabouts, made him look like a scam artist or con man who had learned how to hide from unhappy "customers." Con-men rarely killed. If things got bad, they simply moved on to the next con.

Just then, Paavo heard a soft sound. He switched off his cell phone's flashlight so as not to give his location away. If someone was walking around here, it had to be with a flashlight... or night-vision goggles like the one at the first crime scene.

Scarcely breathing, he listened hard for more sound, wanting to move toward it as soon as he could tell the direction it had come from.

"Oh, my God," Angie cried, running across the laboratory. "Derrick!"

In the center of the lab stood a large metal tub. Derrick lay in it, unconscious, but breathing. On his chest the number seven had been drawn with a marking pen. Angie's eyes took in the implements surrounding him with mounting horror. Butcher knives, a meat cleaver, a hacksaw, power saws, plastic tarps, a meat hook. Suddenly it all came together. She understood what she was seeing. "God help us," she whispered.

Despite her knees going weak, her head light, she somehow found the presence of mind to grab a knife near Derrick and run back to Connie.

They were in the laboratory of the mutilation murderer. Oliver Hardy wasn't the killer after all. The mutilation murderer was still alive... and he planned to kill Derrick... and probably any witnesses to his evil.

Taking hold of the tape covering her friend's mouth, she ripped it off.

"Thank God," Connie whispered as Angie cut through the ropes on her hands and feet. "He wanted me to watch! He gave Derrick some kind of shot to make him unable to move but to stay alive until he bled to death. It was so..." A sob broke. "Then he heard you calling me. That was why he stopped. I don't know what he ran off to do!" She began to cry harder, unable to go on.

Angie couldn't help Derrick yet. If she and Connie didn't get out of there, none of them would escape. She had just freed Connie's ankles and pulled her to her feet when she heard a noise at the door.

The door slowly opened.

Angie's hand tightened on the knife she had used to cut the ropes that held Connie. She hid it behind her back.

A man walked into the lab, removing the night vision goggles that covered his eyes. But even before he did that, even while still wearing the goggles, even though his wig and facial hair were gone, Angie recognized the black turtleneck, the small, gaunt frame.

"Malachi!" she whispered. "Why are you doing this to us? Who are you?"

"I am no man," he said, then laughed. He held a gun in his hand, a large, very lethal-looking handgun with a silencer attached.

At the bizarre words, Angie understood. She gasped, then said, "No man, or *new* man?"

He nodded. "Very good, Angie. Very good. I knew I liked you. Yes, they thought I was dead, the fools. They tried to ruin everything I'd spent my life building. Splitting up the Prometheus Group was a big mistake. Their last mistake. Instead of teaching the world that they walk among us—or, I should say, that *we* walk among *you*—the idiots fight over trivia. They all deserve to die, as does everyone who crossed paths with me at Groom Lake, or as it's better known, Area 51, and didn't listen to me, didn't listen to my warnings!"

"Everyone?" Angie whispered.

"In time, in time. Right now, I have more important things to do. I trust you've looked over my laboratory. Did you notice my laser? Not nearly as good as the one I used at Area 51, but everything there was at least ten years or more ahead of what you civilians use. I enjoyed having Connie in the corner to watch. I'll enjoy you watching even more, Angie."

Angie's voice was strangled. "What are you talking about?"

"The date wasn't finished. Seven-five-forty-seven. I don't have the last seven yet. That was reserved for Holton. He knew it, too. That was why he was scared—why he ran and hid. But he couldn't stay hidden forever. I knew Tardis Hall would lure him back to me, and so it did. Too bad you girls got caught in my trap. Such is life. Or death."

"What about Algernon?"

"He's nothing. The man is a pompous fool, and always has been. But he knows how to lure gullible people to the cause, so I let him hang around me when I had my lab in Area 51. I didn't think he would destroy the Prometheus Group the way he has. He'll pay for it."

"He will?" Angie asked. "He has a book coming out, and these murders will only give him more media attention."

Malachi, a.k.a. I. M. Neumann, chuckled at her words. "You're wrong, Angie. I set up the murders using some old items from my Area 51 laboratories that I knew had his fingerprints. Everyone will think Algernon went mad and killed those men and your precious Derrick Holton. He'll rot in jail the rest of his miserable life. There won't be anything to connect me with this, you see. They all think I'm dead, after all."

"Dr. Mosshad survived. He'll tell what happened."

"He never saw me. Oliver Hardy used chloroform to subdue him and then thought I was caring for Mosshad at his mother's house. I couldn't kill Mosshad—he'd been a friend. So I simply left him tied up with no food or water."

Angie shook her head in disgust.

"But soon, Angie, will come my greatest event ever. I'll go to Treasure Island in the middle of San Francisco Bay. There, I'll flash an enormous hologram of a flying saucer. When the people of San Francisco and on the news see it hovering overhead, ufologists around the world will understand why the bodies had the numbers seven-five-forty-seven."

"They'll connect it to Roswell, you mean?" Angie asked, as she slowly inched away from him, trying to get closer to the door. She still held the knife behind her back, but he had a gun, a very large one.

"It's the most important date in all mankind," he continued. "Christmas Day. The discovery of America. Independence Day. They'll all pale against July 5, 1947. The day the earth was given proof that *we are not alone*. The day my father fell to earth."

He smiled, but then, with eyes red and intense, he suddenly stepped in front of her, blocking her path to the door. "Then, next year, on July 5th, I will let the world know that I am still alive."

"Why are you doing this? Why didn't you let people know you survived the laboratory explosion?"

"I caused the explosion. I needed to 'die' so I could live. As the prophet Malachi once said, so do I: *'If you do not resolve to honor my name, I will send a curse on you...'*"

Angie knew a book of Malachi was in the Bible and now I.M. Neumann was equating himself with a Biblical prophet. "Do you want to run the Prometheus Group again?" she asked.

"Hah. It's nothing. When mankind realizes who and what I am, that I am from the stars, they will beg me to become Lord over the entire earth."

"The only thing they'll realize is that you're crazy," Angie said.

Still wearing a sickly sweet smile, Malachi shook his head. "I've planned this a long, long time. It's the perfect crime. With all the publicity I want. I can hardly wait. Too bad you'll miss it."

Angie and Connie glanced at each other. "Or, you can let us go," Angie suggested. "After all, we watched it all. So we'll be able to tell the world how great you are."

Connie was too petrified to do anything so far, but now, she nodded.

"No, because you'll also tell them I'm a murderer, Angie. I'm not stupid! Right now, there's nothing to link me to the murders. I really quite prefer it this way."

Keep him talking, Angie told herself. Delay. Surely, Paavo and others were searching for her, unless Neumann had somehow stopped them...

"How do I know you're really I. M. Neumann?" she asked, lifting her chin, praying she looked stubborn, defiant. "Everyone says he was killed. I believe them."

Malachi smirked. "I realized your government was my enemy. They sent men in black to kill me because I had found out too much about the important information they hid from the people. So I pretended to be dead as I planned a far greater role for myself."

"But why kill anyone? You could have gone to the public, told your story. You would have been safe."

"You're so naïve, Angie. The public believes whatever the media tells it, and the media is a tool of government. The men I killed had been in Area 51. It was interesting to learn how their exposure to Area 51 had stayed with them over all these years, and when given the slightest encouragement, they sought others who also saw what is out there—things beyond human comprehension. They happily gave my friend, Oliver, their names and addresses."

"So Oliver worked with you?"

"Yes. He was the only one I trusted enough to tell I had returned. He thought he was recruiting old Area 51 workers for me. That was why he believe me when I told him the men who died had been, sadly, killed and mutilated by extra-terrestrials. He helped me wash and move their bodies. He didn't realize what he was really doing until *you* told him the name of the second victim. Then, he questioned what he and I had done."

"And so you killed him?"

"He came to find me, all upset. We went out on the ledge to talk, where no one else would see me. There, the poor boy 'fell.'"

"How did he find you?"

Malachi's lips downturned. "You disappoint me, Angie. Don't you realize I live here in this basement? I even set up my laboratory here. No one has bothered me for years. A few other squatters tried to move in, but they didn't last long. Word quickly got out to stay away from this place. All was fine until the city decided to destroy this building. That meant I had to move, to take action. And here we are."

"Poor Oliver," Angie said.

"Enough of this! I know what you're doing, Angie, and as much as I've enjoyed letting you know how clever I've been, it's over now." He took hold of a rope. "Turn around so I can tie you up. I don't want to hurt you... before I kill you."

Just then, the door to the laboratory sprang open and the man in black burst into the room. Without his sunglasses, finally, Angie could see black, bushy eyebrows over weirdly white eyes. Those eyes found Malachi near Angie and he fired his gun—

Too late.

Malachi had shot first, and the man in black fell onto his back, his arms outstretched. In one hand was a gun, in the other, a flashlight.

As Malachi gawked at what he'd done, Angie immediately raised the knife to stab him, but he turned in time to see it and flung out his arm. The knife pierced his forearm, but did no serious damage.

Still, he screamed in pain and opened his hand, causing his gun to drop. Furious, he turned toward Angie just as Connie swung the meat cleaver he'd planned to use on Derrick at him.

Malachi jumped back, and then slapped her hard in the

face, sending her sprawling as the meat cleaver fell from her hands.

At the same time, Angie dived for his gun.

"You fool!" Malachi bellowed, leaping at her.

The door to the hallway was wide open. Malachi was so close Angie knew she had no time in that long, tight skirt she wore, to pick up the gun, turn and shoot. Instead, hoping against hope some help was out there, she extended her hand toward the gun and shoved it hard, causing it to skid across the concrete floor and out the door into the hallway.

In one rolling movement, Paavo picked it up and, on one knee, aimed at Malachi. "Stop! Or I shoot!" Paavo shouted.

Malachi, reaching for the man in black's firearm, froze. He then slowly raised his hands in the air.

28

An ambulance stood outside Tardis Hall, along with several police cars and one unmarked, black SUV.

Paavo's arm was around Angie as they stood in the parking lot. He was keeping her close, just as he had from the time the police, and others, arrived to help with the situation.

Derrick Holton was in the ambulance and Connie was going with him to San Francisco General Hospital's emergency room. Other than being frightened, she hadn't been hurt.

Malachi/I.M. Neumann was in the custody of the "man in black." The nameless man in black was a government agent. A small, little-known, government agency had been tracking Algernon and the Prometheans for years, checking in now and then to make sure they didn't expose anything important to the public. But as soon the prototype night-vision goggles showed up at the first crime scene, the agency dispatched the man in black and others in the UFO field to watch everyone who was in any way involved with these Roswell-following cults.

Their spying included Angie and her friends.

That night, the agent found Paavo in the basement and told him who he was. Since the agent was armed, he had Paavo stand back a moment as he entered the room, thinking he could easily overpower Malachi. The agent had been wearing a bulletproof vest, so he had only been stunned by the force of the bullet that hit him.

But now, he refused to give Paavo or any of the other San Francisco officers his name or say anything other than to announce he was a Federal special agent. Earlier he had contacted two other Feds to assist him. They had now arrived, handcuffed Malachi, and placed him in an unmarked black SUV.

The man in black then informed Paavo, Angie, and Connie, before she left with Derrick, that they "hadn't seen what they had seen." He said he was taking "crazy but brilliant" Malachi with him, and everything they "thought" had happened that night, hadn't happened. Malachi had set up a "mini-Area 51" in the basement with strange, old implements he'd taken before he blew up his laboratory years earlier. Even then, Malachi believed he was smarter than mere earthlings and shouldn't be working for them, but should rule them.

The government would now take charge of cleaning up Malachi's Tardis Hall laboratory, and moving everything he had out of there.

"What about the fact that Malachi killed four men and planned more killings?" Paavo asked the agent.

"I believe it's been documented that John Oliver Harding, a suicide, was the killer of the three men," the man in black announced. "No sense reopening the case. Besides, I. M. Neumann is dead, and this Malachi, we don't know he even exists, right? Plus, we'll talk to Professor Holton and Dr. Mosshad. Believe me, neither of them will be pressing charges."

"Why not?" Angie called out.

The agent looked coldly at her and without reply, turned to leave.

"Wait!" Paavo insisted. "You can't just walk off with our suspect. What he did here is a state crime, not federal."

"Theoretically, you're right. But don't try to stop us. We'll be in touch." He then got into the black SUV with the other agents and Malachi, and they left.

The arm Angie had around Paavo's waist tightened as she asked, "Do you believe he'll bring Malachi back for trial?"

He frowned. "Not one bit."

Both the ambulance and the black SUV left the parking lot, Derrick's ambulance turned in the direction of the hospital, while the SUV with Malachi turned south, in the direction of the airport.

Angie then let go of Paavo, and squared her shoulders. "I guess I had better go back inside to pack up my dishes and get out of here," she said. "I've had quite enough of this place. Did Algernon ever show up?"

"Not that I saw. I doubt anyone will care much about him once news of this gets out," Paavo said as he faced her. From the time he'd stopped Malachi, this was the first time they'd been alone. His hand lightly brushed a lock of hair that had fallen to near the huge brown eyes he loved to look into. The fear he'd felt at the sound of a gunshot, the site of a killer trying to grab hold of her as she lay on the ground, proved to him—not that he needed it—how much he cared about her.

"Are you all right to go back in there alone?" he asked. "I've got to take care of a couple of things out here, and then I can go in with you and help."

She gazed up at him with love in her eyes, but then quickly dropped her gaze. "Earl, Butch, and Vinnie are probably still inside, guarding the food. I'll be okay."

He nodded, then watched her walk away.

"What the hell's going on here?" Algernon got out of Triana Crisswell's Mercedes and now stood in the nearly empty parking lot, flapping his arms and staring at what should have been a festive event. He had watched an ambulance pull out of the parking lot, along with a few other cars. Only two police cars were left in it, plus a few nondescript cars, and Angie's Ferrari. "What happened to my huge book signing, Triana?"

Triana stood beside her car and folded her arms. "I told you we should have gotten here on time, but noooo. You wanted to be late so people would be clamoring to see you. Looks like they clamored themselves into a riot or something! Let's go talk to the police about what happened."

She started toward the group, but Algernon stopped her. "No! Stop! Let's leave them alone. Who cares what happened? The bottom line is my event is ruined." He folded his arms and glared at her. "I thought you could put on a simple little publicity gala. Obviously, I was wrong."

"I had nothing to do with whatever happened here tonight!" Triana shrieked. "Besides, people were calling all day long with one excuse after the other not to attend after the news about that murderous lunatic, Oliver Hardy! Maybe only trouble makers showed up. Frankly, at this point, I don't see that it matters."

"What do you mean, it doesn't matter?" He raged. "It matters to me! To my book, my career! What kind of imbecile are you?"

She stiffened her spine. "You don't have to get nasty! This is hardly my fault."

"Not your fault? Whose is it, then? What a fiasco! It's *all* your fault. You and that Fantasy Dinner woman you hired who didn't even appreciate all I planned to do for her."

Triana arched an eyebrow. "Oh? And what did you plan to do for her?"

"I—" He snapped his mouth shut, his eyes darting. "Nothing."

"I thought you were a little too interested in her!" Triana yelled.

"Me?" he asked, wide-eyed.

"Don't play innocent, you, you, you playboy! Not to mention what the food for this non-existent party will cost me. If my husband finds out I've spent more money on you, he'll be madder than ever. Now, I learn you were trying to mess around with the hired help!"

"Miss Amalfi is hardly in the category of hired help, Triana," he said, unable to stop a smile from touching his lips as he thought of Angie.

"You old goat!" she ranted. "You're old enough to be her father. Those facelifts haven't erased years, only wrinkles!" She turned and marched toward her car.

"Triana, you're being unreasonable." He followed her.

"The only thing unreasonable about me was paying attention to you in the first place. See how far you get without me—and my money! And if you think I'm going to pay for any of this, you've got another think coming! You can pay your 'Miss Amalfi' yourself! Goodbye."

She got into her big Mercedes and locked the doors.

He clutched the door handle. "Triana, wait! I can't pay her! Unlock the door, please! You aren't going to leave me out here in this neighborhood at night, are you?"

She gunned the engine and took off. He ran after her, waving his arms and shouting for her to stop.

29

It had taken Angie and "the boys," as she called them, little time to take down the decorations, pack up Angie's warming and other plates—the food was all gone—and put them in her car.

It took Paavo a lot longer than he expected to deal with the immediate fallout of events at Tardis Hall, so he had suggested she go home and he'd stop by to see her as soon he could.

Now, Angie sat alone in her apartment, still a little shell-shocked over all that had taken place. She had taken off her silly 1940s outfit and put on comfortable lounging pajamas, expecting it would be a long night. Connie had phoned her to say the doctors gave Derrick something to counteract the injection Malachi had given him, and he should have no lingering effects from his near-death experience. At least, no lasting physical effects.

The clock was approaching midnight before Angie heard the familiar knock on her door, although much softer than usual due to the late hour.

She opened the door, but didn't say a word, wondering if Paavo was going to rush off the way he'd been doing lately.

"I didn't wake you, did I?" he asked.

"No. I was hoping you'd stop by, as you'd said." She took a deep breath, then ventured, "would you like to come in?"

"Sure," he said. He went to the sofa, removed his jacket and gun, which she took as a good sign.

"Can I get you anything? Coffee? A beer?"

"No thanks." He sat on the sofa.

She sat on the nearby easy chair.

"I'm sorry about what happened to your first Fantasy Dinner," he said. "It looked like it should have been a great event. You worked hard at it, and I hope you aren't feeling too discouraged."

"Thank you for that. But this isn't the business for me. I realized that a while back, but felt obligated to put on the event." She gave a weighty sigh. "I'll come up with something, eventually."

"I know you will. Maybe something more 'down-to-earth'?"

She smiled at that. "So true. I don't want any more fantasies, either. UFOs and aliens have cured me of that."

"Don't remind me," he said. "I'm still pissed off about the way that man in black character took off with Malachi or Neumann or whatever his name really is."

"Well, whoever he is, I'm not impressed," Angie said. "If he'd been watching more closely, Malachi wouldn't have managed four murders, and almost more. Even tonight, you saved us, not him."

"I couldn't have done any of it without your help," he said with a smile. "Your timing in knocking the gun to me in the hallway was perfection. How did you know I was out there?"

"I didn't. But I knew, if you were near, you could use it."

"You had that right."

"Glad to be of service."

But then, Angie felt it was time to change the subject. "At

least Derrick is doing well." She told him about Connie's phone call.

"I wish Connie well with him and his UFO beliefs," Paavo said. "At least he's one old boyfriend your father won't want to trade me in for."

She eyed him. "That really bothered you, didn't it?"

He grimaced. "I know I'm not the kind of man your father expects for you. I also know he's right about that."

As much as she hated to ruin the peace that had settled on them after the earlier turmoil and terror, she couldn't simply let his words rest. "I'm sorry you feel that way. Is my father the reason you don't want to see me anymore? Or was it something I did? You've made your feelings clear, but don't I deserve to know why?"

He looked surprised by her words, but then dropped his gaze a long moment. Finally, he spoke, his voice soft. "You do deserve to know. And it's not because of you, and definitely not because of your father. It's about me."

She braced herself. That, she feared, was the worst possibility. She might have been able to fix what he didn't like that she was doing, and she could have explained away issues about her father. But if he no longer cared about her, or if he'd met someone else, it was hopeless. "I see," she whispered.

"I realized," he began slowly, "that in the course of my prior two cases, big, deadly cases, I'd put you in danger. It was my fault, Angie. In the case just before this one, you were within seconds of being killed. The case before it, you met Axel Klaw —a dangerous man. My own sister died because of him. And now, because of me, he knows who you are, and where you live." He shook his head. "I can't do that to you. Not anymore. I've always been a loner, as you know. Now, I understand why. It's best this way."

Angie rubbed her forehead. Every pore in her cried out that he was wrong to feel that way, but knowing Paavo, emotions wouldn't work. He was analytical, fact based, which was what made him such a good homicide investigator.

"You realize, of course, that my involvement in this latest case was because of my business, and had nothing to do with your job," she said.

"Yes, of course, but—"

"And you know, if you hadn't been in the basement trying to find me, I'd be dead now."

He shut his eyes a moment. "Angie, that's not the point."

"Isn't it? It's the way I see it, which seems every bit as valid as the way you see things."

"I'm trying to keep you safe. You... you get involved in things. The guys in the Homicide have picked up on it. They know, as I do, you put yourself in danger. I can't be responsible for you doing that."

"Of course you aren't responsible." Her voice was firm. "Paavo, I'll always do what I want, whether you want to be with me or not."

He shook his head. "Still—"

"Tell me," she continued, "is there some statistic out there that says how many 'significant others' of police officers, men or women, are killed because of their relationship?"

"Well, no, but—"

"No? That's your answer?" Doing all she could to keep her voice calm, she continued. "So, you've made up this idea in your head that I'm not safe being around you, based on nothing, when to be factual, you've actually kept me safe. And, let me remind you, at least once, I saved your life as well. Is that not true?"

"Yes, but—"

"Stop." She stood. "I'm going up to my deck. It's a beautiful night and after all this UFO stuff, I think looking at real stars is what I need to do right now." She faced him, then drew in her breath. "It's up to you. I can't be 'just friends' with you. I tried it, but it's simply too painful for me. Either we're together, or we're not. But you need to decide honestly and truthfully." She walked toward the back door that led up to the deck that came with her penthouse apartment, then she looked back at him, maybe seeing him in her apartment for the last time. "You can join me, or you can leave."

A balmy breeze came in from the bay as Angie reached her rooftop deck. She rarely went up there and had never done much with the space. It had rattan chairs usually kept in an enclosure to protect them from wind, fog, and rain.

She pulled out a couple of chairs, but didn't sit. Instead she stood and looked up at the night sky. The building was tall enough that little of the city's lights reached it. Without the fog or the omnipresent city glare, the stars seemed brighter, with far more of them visible than usual. The moon was a mere sliver.

She waited and waited, and when her hope was all but gone and she was about to give up, she heard his footsteps. Her heartbeat quickened. He reached the roof and walked toward her, then stopped.

She faced him, scarcely breathing.

"This is how the stars should be enjoyed," Paavo said as he stepped to her side.

"Is it?" she whispered.

"I think so." He seemed to study her a long moment. "Who knows what mysteries may be out there? But the one thing we can be sure of, is that what's visible to us, is wondrous."

His words, and the way he looked at her, filled her. She knew what his joining her meant. He didn't need to say it, and neither did she.

Through his words, Angie saw a side of her tough detective

she rarely glimpsed—a man moved by the profound beauty of the universe. But when he turned those pale blue eyes toward her, what she saw in them moved her so deeply, she could no longer keep her feelings secret. "I want you to know, Inspector Smith, I do love you so very, very much."

"Angie." He whispered her name as if it were a caress.

Then, in keeping with the way she had addressed him, he added, "And I love you, Miss Amalfi,"—his voice was low and heartfelt as he drew her into his arms—"more than all the stars in the sky."

And then, finally, he kissed her.

ABOUT THE AUTHOR

Joanne Pence was born and raised in northern California and now lives in Idaho. She has been an award-winning, *USA Today* best-selling author of mysteries for many years, but she has also written historical fiction, contemporary romance, romantic suspense, a fantasy, and supernatural suspense. All of her books are now available as ebooks and in print, and most are also offered in special large print editions. Joanne hopes you'll enjoy her books, which present a variety of times, places, and reading experiences, from mysterious to thrilling, emotional to lightly humorous, as well as powerful tales of times long past.

Visit her at www.joannepence.com and be sure to sign up for Joanne's mailing list to hear about new books.

Milton Keynes UK
Ingram Content Group UK Ltd.
UKHW010937110724
445228UK00004B/259